DOMINIC

One day hound Dominic sets out on the high road going nowhere in particular. He's just moving along, on his way to wherever he gets, to find whatever he finds. And that's plenty: a witch-alligator full of advice, the dreaded Doomsday Gang, an invalid pig who leaves Dominic his fortune, a goose somewhat curiously named Matilda Fox, an elephant who *has* forgotten, and a host of other engaging characters, all of whom involve Dominic in adventures. A splendidly different sort of fairytale for readers of nine upwards.

'The book is a sheer delight.'
Margery Fisher, The Sunday Times

William Steig

DOMINIC

COLLINS · LIONS

First published in Great Britain 1973 by Hamish Hamilton
First published in Lions 1974
by William Collins Sons & Co Ltd
14 St James's Place, London SW1

© 1972 by William Steig

Printed in Great Britain
C. Nicholls & Company Ltd.

*This book was written at the behest of
Michael di Capua and it is dedicated to him
as well as to Maggie and Melinda*

DOMINIC

I. Dominic was a lively one, always up to something. One day, more restless than usual, he decided there wasn't enough going on in his own neighbourhood to satisfy his need for adventure. He just had to get away.

He owned an assortment of hats which he liked to wear, not for warmth or for shade or to shield him from rain, but for their various effects—rakish, dashing, solemn, or martial. He packed them, together with his precious piccolo and a few other things, in a large bandanna which he tied to the end of a stick so it could be carried easily over a shoulder.

Too impatient to dash around saying goodbye to everyone, he hammered this note to his door: "Dear Friends, I am leaving in rather a hurry to see more of the world, so I have no time to say goodbye to you individually. I embrace you all and sniff you with love. I don't know when I'll be back. But back I will be. Dominic."

He locked the door, buried the key, and left home to seek his fortune—that is, to look for whatever it was that was going to happen to him out there in the unknown world.

He took the highroad going east so he could greet the sunrise as soon as it arrived, and also the nightfall. But he didn't travel in a straight line. He was forever leaving the road, coming back to it and leaving it again, investigating the source of every smell and sound, every sight that intrigued him. Nothing escaped his ardent attention.

On the second day of his journey, he reached a fork in the road and he wondered whether to go the way that veered off to the left or the one that curved over to the right. He would have been happy to go both ways at once. Since that was impossible, he flipped a coin—heads for the left, tails for the right. It fell on tails, so he chased his own tail three times around and took the road that curved over to the right.

By and by, there was an exceptional smell, one he had never encountered before, and hurrying toward it, as he always hurried toward every development, he came to another fork in the road, and there a witch-alligator stood, resting on a cane and looking as if she had been expecting him.

Dominic had never seen a witch-alligator. Though all smells engaged his interest, he wasn't sure he liked her particular one, and it seemed to him that she had many more teeth than were necessary for any ordinary dental purpose. Still, he greeted her in his usual

high-spirited way: "Good morning! Happy day to us all!"

"Good morning to you," said the witch. "Do you know where you're going?"

"Not at all," Dominic said with a laugh. "I'm going wherever my fortune tells me to go."

"And would you like to know your fortune?" the witch asked, adjusting the fringes on her shawl. "I can see the future just as clearly as I see the present and more clearly than I can recall the past. For twenty-five cents I'll reveal your immediate prospects —what is in store for you during the next few days. For half a dollar I'll describe the next full year of your life. For a dollar you can have your complete history, unexpurgated, from now to the finish."

Dominic thought a moment. Curious as he was about everything, especially everything concerning himself, he preferred to do his own learning. "I'm

certainly interested in my fortune," he said. "Yet I think it would be much more fun to find out what happens when it happens. I like to be taken by surprise."

"Well," said the witch, "I know everything that's going to happen to you." Then she remarked that Dominic was unusually wise for so young a dog and offered him a bit of information. "I hope you don't mind if I tell you this much," she said. "That road there on the right goes nowhere. There's not a bit of magic up that road, no adventure, no surprise, nothing to discover or wonder at. Even the scenery is humdrum.

You'd soon grow much too introspective. You'd take to daydreaming and tail-twiddling, get absent-minded and lazy, forget where you are and what you're about, sleep more than one should, and be wretchedly bored. Furthermore, after a while, you'd reach a dead end and you'd have to come all that dreary way back to right here where we're standing now, only it wouldn't be now, it would be some woefully wasted time later.

"Now this road, the one on the left," she said, her heavy eyes glowing, "this road keeps right on going, as far as anyone cares to go, and if you take it, believe me, you'll never find yourself wondering what you might have missed by not taking the other. Up this road, which looks the same at the beginning, but is really ever so different, things will happen that you never could have guessed at—marvellous, unbelievable things. Up this way is where adventure is. I'm pretty sure I know which way you'll go." And she smiled, exposing all eighty teeth.

Dominic feverishly opened his big, polka-dotted bandanna, pulled out some sardines, and gave them to the witch, who consumed them in a gulp. He thanked her for her good advice and went high-tailing it up the road to the left, the road to adventure.

II. The adventure road started out through a shady wood. On both sides the trees stood tall and solemn. The light glowed greenly through their leaves as if through stained-glass windows in a church. Dominic walked along in silence, smelling all the wonderful forest odours, alert to every new one, his nostrils quivering with delight. He smelled damp earth, mushrooms, dried leaves, violets, mint, spruce, rotting wood, animal droppings, forget-me-nots, and mould, and he savoured all of it. The odours came as single notes, or percussion shots, or fused together in wonderful harmonies. Dominic was inspired to take out his piccolo and play. He invented a melody which he decided should be called "The Psalm of Sweet Smells."

Presently he came to a quiet pond. Putting away

his piccolo, he reconnoitred the grassy bank, investigating various plants, pebbles, and anthills, and then sat down to enjoy some lunch. Scarcely had he wolfed a couple of sardines than the smooth surface of the pond before him ruffled and there was a huge catfish regarding him with unblinking eyes.

"You're Dominic," the catfish said.

Dominic was aquiver with attention. "Yes, I'm Dominic," he admitted. "Who are you?"

"I can't tell you my name," said the catfish. "But I have something for you. I've been waiting for you to pass by so I could give it to you." And he held forth out of the water a long, sharp spear. "You're going to need this," he said. "This fine-edged spear will make you invincible in serious combat. That is, if you use it rightly."

"What is 'using it rightly'?" Dominic asked, accepting the spear.

"Using it rightly," said the fish, "is using it with such skill that no one can best you."

"I see," said Dominic. "Thank you very much."

"You needn't thank me," said the fish. "I'm acting on orders." And he disappeared, leaving behind a small ripple that also disappeared.

Dominic never did find out whose orders the catfish was acting on. He speculated that it was the witch.

Remembering the fish, he felt guilty for having eaten sardines. But he quickly got over it and ate

another. He discarded the stick that had served to carry his bandanna and replaced it with the spear. Then he put on his Royal Fusiliers hat and continued on his way.

In not many minutes, proving that the witch had been correct when she said there would be action along this road, he fell into a deep hole. He looked up from the bottom. And, proving that the catfish had been right when he said Dominic would need the spear, he saw three masked faces looking down at him. They belonged to members of the Doomsday Gang.

The Doomsday Gang robbed, ravaged, cheated, attacked innocent creatures at large and travellers especially, and did all sorts of damaging mischief; and the hole into which Dominic had fallen was a trap they had set for anyone at all who might happen to be passing that way. Dominic hadn't seen the hole because it had been cleverly covered with burdock leaves, arranged to look as if they had fallen there by chance.

III.

"Well, look what we've caught!" said the fox who was captain of the gang. "I think we've got a good one, a real prize." And he laughed.

"I'll bet he has a slew of fine things in that fat bandanna," said the ferret crouching next to him. "It looks full as a ripe melon."

"I wonder if he's good to eat," said the third character looking down the hole, a weasel.

"No, their meat is tough," said the fox. "But surely we can use him for something or other. Maybe for hunting. They have an incredible sense of smell."

These villains were never really certain what they wanted. But they knew they liked to be evil, in any convenient way. Being evil was what they were best at; everyone enjoys being best at something.

"They make too much noise," said the ferret,

whereupon Dominic vented a series of ear-tearing barks. Then to frighten them he growled, but they didn't scare.

"Let's get him now," said the fox, and the three started edging into the hole.

"Stand back! Stand back there!" commanded Dominic, and without waiting for a response, he jabbed, jabbed, jabbed at them with his long, sharp spear.

"Ouch!" said the ferret, though he hadn't been touched. "Oops," said the weasel. "Curses!" said the fox. They strove to get at him with sticks and clubs and swords, but Dominic held them at bay with the wonderful weapon the catfish had given him.

They were clever as only a fox and a ferret and a weasel can be, but they were no match for Dominic's busy spear. They tried to knock it out of his grip, but Dominic was too quick for them, too adroit, and he knew no fear.

"Shall we get some help?" asked the weasel, flustered.

"No," said the fox, "we'll wear him out soon. The way he's going, he's bound to get tired." But they didn't know Dominic. By the time night came, it was the Doomsday Gang that was worn out, not he. Dominic's strength was increasing. Action always inspired him. He poked and jabbed his spear with increasing skill and abandon.

"I don't think we can get to him just yet," said the fox. "We can keep him down in the hole, but we can't get him. Let's sleep now, and in the morning he's ours. He'll be up all night worrying, while we're resting, and then it'll be child's play to deal with him."

The ferret and the weasel agreed. They invariably agreed with the fox, but it wouldn't have mattered if they had disagreed. The fox always had his way with them. Besides, they were tired. Laughing at the futility of Dominic's position, they covered the hole with logs, and after some more cruel jesting, they fell asleep on them, confident of success in the morning.

Down in the hole, which was now getting a bit stuffy, what with the logs covering it, Dominic wasn't a bit worried. Challenges were his delight. Whatever life offered was, this way or that, a test of one's skills, one's faculties; and he enjoyed proving equal to these tests.

With three villains sleeping on the logs above him,

there was no way he could get out of the hole. That was plain. What would you do if you were in Dominic's predicament? Well, that's exactly what Dominic did. He began putting to use his great talent for digging. He clawed away at the side of the hole while his enemies were lost in their nasty dreams.

So steadily and swiftly did Dominic dig, and so cleverly did he shift the displaced earth, that it was not too long before he had room enough to work his spear around in the right direction and dig with it too. Working away, he was happy he had gone out into the world to seek his fortune. So many interest-

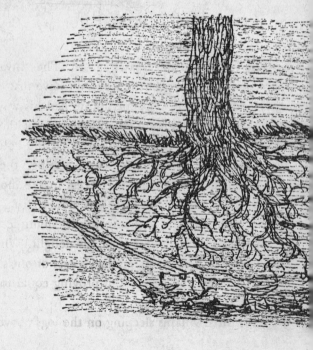

ing things to do! With four sets of claws and the spear, and a bountiful supply of energy, he burrowed a long tunnel away from the hole and under the crowded roots of a large tree. Then he worked his way upward to the surface.

Just before dawn he was standing on grass, several yards distant from the slumbering Doomsday Gang. He could hear the fox softly snoring, the ferret licking his chops. Excited by his successful exertions, Dominic couldn't help letting out one short bark to announce his liberation.

This of course awakened the fox, the ferret, and

the weasel. The earth was now barely supporting the logs and them, and at their first sudden movements of surprise, they tumbled, snarling and clawing at one another, into the hole they themselves had dug.

Meanwhile, Dominic, more enthusiastic for adventure than ever, set out on the road again, all his senses alert.

IV. The dawn came up rosy and young. Striding along, Dominic was decidedly glad to be free. But the labours of the night began to tell on him. Dog-tired, he flung himself down at the edge of the road and sighed a powerful sigh. After a fidget or two, he fell asleep, when everyone else in the surrounding world was just waking up.

It was a refreshing sleep. In his dreams he relived the adventures of the night that had just turned to morning. He was in the hole again, digging with claws and with spear, aware of the villains sleeping above him. A yelp stirred in his throat but he quickly stifled it, knowing even in his dream that he had to dig the burrow silently.

The dream was ended by the frantic buzzing of a yellow wasp struggling in a spider's web strung among the branches of the bush behind him. The instant he heard that unique sound he leaped away, even before he was fully conscious. He had once been stung by a yellow jacket, right on the snout, while smelling some peonies. Enough of that kind of experience! He had had to soak his snout in cold mud for over an hour before the pain even considered subsiding.

The sight of the yellow jacket striving to free itself, however, aroused Dominic's pity. And he didn't like spiders, especially when they moved—with all those extra legs. He didn't want to get stung and he knew he was safe while the wasp was trussed up in spider strings, but his passionate love of liberty won out. He took his good spear, and standing as far from the web as he could, he cut the wasp free. Then he quickly backed away and kept on backing.

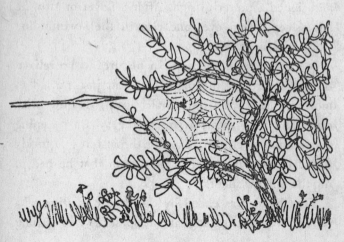

The freed yellow jacket followed him, circling again and again above his head. Dominic, watching his strange movements, saw him swoop, dip, spell out the words

Thank you

in invisible skywriting and disappear in the shimmering blue air.

By way of breakfast Dominic ate some mushrooms, a sprig of mint, and a bit of wild garlic. Then he donned his mountain-climbing hat, the one with a green feather in it, shouldered his spear with the bandanna securely tied to the end, and was off once more on his travels.

V. "What a wonderful world!" thought Dominic. "How perfect!" Had it been up to him when things were first made, he wouldn't have made them a whit different. Every leaf was in its proper place. Pebbles, stones, flowers, all were just as they ought to be. Water ran where water should run. The sky was properly blue. All sounds were in tune. Everything had its appropriate smell. Dominic was master of himself and in accord with the world. He was perfectly happy.

Rounding a bend, he saw smoke properly curling from a proper chimney, and under the chimney he saw a strange little house, perfectly, properly strange. He decided to visit and share a spot of tea, perhaps, with whoever it was who lived inside. He never debated these impulses, hemming and hawing over what he should do. Thought and action were not separate with Dominic; the moment he thought to do something, he was already doing it. So he knocked at the door and listened for an answer. A weak voice asked, "Who's there?"

"It's me, Dominic," said Dominic.

"Who's Dominic?" asked the weak voice, with a quaver.

"I'm a traveller on this road and I'd like to say hello and pass the time of day with whoever you are there inside this charming house."

"You're probably one of the Doomsday Gang," said the one inside, "and you're using an affected voice, trying to sound like a dog. And your friends are right there behind you—I can almost see them."

"No, no, I'm Dominic! I'll bark to prove it." And he barked.

"Show your face at the window," said the voice inside. Dominic dashed to the window and, standing up on his toes, placed his front paws lightly on the sill and peered in. He saw a very old, very wrinkled pig, very unpink and unwell-looking, lying in bed; he was sunk deep in pillows and covered with the craziest crazy-quilt Dominic had ever seen. On the stove, not far from the bed, a kettle was steaming. And of course

the pig, looking out through bleary eyes, saw Dominic. "Come in," he said. "There's a key under that flowerpot by the left side of the door."

Dominic entered. "Lock the door, please," said the pig, and Dominic did. Dominic always noticed smells first. The room smelled like a sickroom. The air was stale. And the pig smelled like a sick pig. Dominic went over to the bed and sat near him.

"I'm sorry you're not feeling well," he said.

"I'm not just 'not feeling well,'" said the pig, "I'm

feeling miserable. I barely had enough strength to light the fire and put that kettle on to boil. Tea always cheers me up. I wanted some."

"So did I," said Dominic. "I'll make it. Just you lie there and be comfortable." He smelled out where the tea was. He also smelled out the sugar and the milk. And while he was at it, he smelled out some corn muffins and marmalade, and some partridge eggs, which he scrambled with a bit of fresh parsley.

Dominic's briskness was heartening to the sick old pig. His spirits livened. "How lucky, how very lucky I am that you passed by on this road. Where are you going, if I may ask?"

"No place in particular," said Dominic. "I'm just moving along, on my way to wherever I get, to find whatever I find."

"Well, I hope you don't find the Doomsday Gang," said the pig.

"It may be that I have already," said Dominic. And he told about the fox, the weasel, and the ferret who had had him trapped, so they thought, down in the hole.

"That's them all right," muttered the pig. "That's part of the gang."

"Well, I'm not afraid of them," said Dominic, as he served the pig his tea and food and quickly fell to eating his own. It would be hard to say who ate with better manners, the pig or Dominic. Each had his own style, his own way of dealing with an egg, his own way of handling a teacup and taking his tea. The pig expressed the opinion that Dominic prepared food as well as the subtlest chef. Dominic blushed under his fur.

"Tell me about yourself," he said as he cleared away the dishes. The food had commanded all his attention, but now he was curious about his host.

"All right," said the pig, "sit by my side. I tire easily and I can't talk while you're busying about." Dominic made himself comfortable at the pig's side.

"My name," said the pig, "is Badger. Bartholomew Badger. Now don't ask how a family of pigs got the name Badger. I don't know. And my father and my grandfather didn't know. The name goes way back . . . I'm a hundred years old. If I were to tell you the whole story of my life, being hardly able to lift my jowls to talk, it might take another hundred years telling it. I'll tell you just a few things." But talking that much had made the pig so tired he fell asleep.

Dominic washed him with rubbing alcohol while he slept. He opened all the windows to let in fresh air and let out the stale. Then he went outside and picked a cheerful bouquet of wild flowers, wild enough to have no names, and arranged them in a lovely vase on Mr. Badger's bed table.

When he woke up, he began talking again, as though he wasn't aware he had ever stopped. "I'm all alone in the world and I feel I haven't got much longer to live. I've had a very interesting life. I wish I could tell you about all the wonderful things that have happened to me, all the strange things I've seen, all the exciting adventures I've had. I hope you have . . ." Mr. Badger dozed off again. A bluebottle fly buzzed around his snoring snout. Dominic brushed it away.

After an hour's nap, the pig woke and continued:

". . . as good a life. It used to be very peaceful around here; it was just as happy a place as you could wish for. But now everyone lives behind bolted doors and is always on guard against unexpected developments. Did I say 'unexpected'? They *are* expected. It's that rotten Doomsday Gang. Heaven knows where they came from, how they got started. But they ply up and down this road doing nothing but harm, keeping everyone anxious and worried.

"When I was younger, I had no problem with them. They were afraid of me. I was a pretty powerful pig, if I say so myself. But now that I'm old and feeble, they're always trying to get in here and take whatever they fancy. I wish I had my young strength just for a day to deal with them as they should be dealt with. You'd see some fur fly!"

Mr. Badger got so emotionally wrought up when he said this that he shook all over. This made the bed rattle and the whole house seemed to tremble with his rage. Dominic had to calm him down. He told him he'd keep a lookout and make sure no one got in the house. He locked all the doors and windows, and remembering the story of the Three Little Pigs, he rekindled the fire in the fireplace so no one could come down the chimney.

Mr. Badger fell asleep again. The house got overly warm. Dominic fell asleep too. Both he and the pig dreamed about heat, about a broiling sun, live embers, steaming vapours, molten lava.

VI. For the next several days Dominic was Mr. Badger's nurse, housekeeper, and friend. He fed him well. He kept his house clean and neat; he talked to him and listened to him talk. He kept him warm when he felt cold and he fanned him when he was too warm. Most helpful of all was the music he played on his piccolo. It brought peace to the pig's spirit.

One day Mr. Badger asked Dominic to sit beside him for a serious talk. "Dominic," he said, "Dominic, my friend—you *are* my friend even though we've known each other only a few days . . . Dominic, I know my time has come to leave this life. I've lived a hundred years, and I'm not going to live any longer. I'm at the end of the story entitled Bartholomew Badger. As I've told you, I'm alone in the world. I've had many relatives, many friends, all dear to me, but they all passed on before me. I was my mother's youngest child, the baby of the family."

As Mr. Badger paused to rest, Dominic tried to visualize him as a baby, but he could only imagine a tiny pig looking old and wrinkled. Mr. Badger continued: "I was happily married, very much in love with my wife, and prosperous, but we never had any children. It was the one thing missing from our life. How we longed to have piglets of our own! Of course we enjoyed playing with the children of others, but it wasn't the same as having our own. Dominic, I hope for your sake you will have a lot of children. But now I want to talk of something more immediate. Just a moment, let me catch my breath." Something that had to be said was on his mind. "Dominic, please get me a shot of brandy, so I can go on talking."

Dominic got Mr. Badger a jigger of applejack and had some himself. It was strong stuff and he had to growl to clear the burning in his throat. "Dominic, let me continue. That sneaking gang of thieves and cut-throats hasn't just been after the things you see around this house. They know I'm extremely wealthy —and now you know it—and they want my wealth. But they're not going to get their filthy paws on it. It's buried, and the only one who knows where it's buried is me. These Doomsday devils have tried every possible trick to pry my secret loose. They even spent a whole day preaching charity to me, one at each window shouting pious messages. But I've lived long enough, goodness knows, to understand that sort of play-acting."

Mr. Badger looked warmly at Dominic. "Dominic," he said, resting his hoof on Dominic's paw, "I want *you* to inherit my wealth."

Dominic was taken aback. "No, no," he protested, "I didn't help you so I'd get anything. I helped you because you needed help. Besides, you're not going to die!"

"I am," said Bartholomew Badger, "as sure as this is Wednesday the fourteenth, I am." Dominic looked at the calendar. It was Wednesday the fourteenth. "I know you didn't help me with a reward in mind. Anyway, this is no reward. I am leaving my entire estate, all my assets, to you. Period. You've seen that pear tree at the back of the house. Stand at the pear tree facing due south. Walk one hundred and three paces and you will come to four black stones laid together in the form of a square. Remove the stones and dig. It's yours, all of it."

"Keep your money," said Dominic. "I don't want it. I only want you to stay alive and get well. I'll bet you could live another hundred years!"

"Nonsense," said the pig, looking very, very tired. "I don't know just when I'm going. I'll say goodbye now. I'm so happy to have known you and so grateful for your kindness. Now, please, play me something beautiful on your piccolo."

Dominic played his piccolo. He played quite a while, and while he played, Bartholomew Badger passed into the next world with a peaceful smile on his face. Dominic, worried, tried to wake him; then he realized the pig was dead.

VII.
Dominic went out for a long walk and did a lot of thinking. He was still walking when the stars came out. Mournful, he lay down on the ground and looked at the stars. Life was mysterious. Bartholomew Badger had been alive long before there was a Dominic—long before anybody had even thought there would ever be such a dog. Two hours ago Bartholomew Badger was still alive. But now he was gone. There was no Bartholomew Badger; there was only a memory. His turn was over. Dominic's turn was still at the beginning. There were many who hadn't yet even begun to exist, but there they would be, some time in the future, a whole new world of creatures, some important, some not, and many of them wondering about life just as Dominic was wondering now. It would be their turn, and then Domi-

nic's turn would be over. Many of them would think about the past, which was now the present, but by then what was now the future would have become the present.

Somehow this kind of thinking made Dominic feel more religious than usual. He fell asleep under the vast dome of quivering stars, and just as he was falling asleep, passing over into the phase of dreams, he felt he understood the secret of life. But in the light of morning, when he woke up, his understanding of the secret had disappeared with the stars. The mystery was still there, inspiring his wonder.

He returned to the house. He was not of a mind to eat breakfast. He was not in the mood. He went to the tool shed to get Mr. Badger's shovel, and he laboured in the morning sun, digging a deep hole. He dug the hole under a tall oak tree, as old as Mr. Badger, in the front yard; and he buried the pig in the hole.

Then he leaned on the shovel to rest, the wooden handle warm with his work. The moment he stopped being busy, he felt his heart quake. He had to cry. Life was suddenly too sad. And yet it was beautiful. The beauty was dimmed when the sadness welled up. And the beauty would be there again when the sadness went. So the beauty and the sadness belonged together somehow, though they were not the same at all.

Dominic couldn't abide being in the doldrums for

long. The doldrums were dreary, and Dominic's spirit was sprightly, it liked to rollick. So he had to get moving. He shook off the dumps, and since he was still holding the shovel with which he had buried Mr. Badger, he went to dig up the treasure.

He walked to the pear tree at the back of the house, got his bearings from a weather vane on the roof which showed the four main directions of the world, and faced due south, with his back to the tree. Then he carefully marked off one hundred and three paces and stopped to look for the four stones forming a square that the pig had described. They weren't there.

Perhaps he had made a mistake. Be calm. He went back to the pear tree, made sure he was facing in the right direction, and paced off one hundred three paces again. Again there were no stones. He sat down to think. "Aha! When Mr. Badger was talking about paces," he thought, "he was talking about his own paces, pig paces, not dog paces!" He jumped up, returned to the pear tree once more, counted off one hundred and three paces, and kept going due south. At one hundred and fifty-one Dominic paces he found the four black stones Mr. Badger had spoken of. He removed them and dug.

Below the topsoil his shovel struck something hard. It turned out to be a small chest encircled by riveted metal bands. He dragged it out by its iron handle and opened it. It was brimful of precious pearls. Above all else the pig had cherished pearls and they were the last things he'd committed to the ground. Farther down was a second chest, a little bigger than the first. Dominic broke the lock open by hitting it with a rock. The chest was chock-full of diamonds, rubies, emeralds, amethysts, sapphires, alexandrite, garnets, and other precious stones, all in the form of brilliant necklaces, rings, earrings, nose rings, brooches, bracelets, lockets, and bangles; and when these objects lay exposed in the open sunlight, clear, crystalline sparks of vivid light slashed off in all directions.

Dominic marvelled at the spectacle. He dug still farther. At the bottom of the hole, down in the hardpan, was a leather sack swollen with gold pieces. There was something else in the sack. As if to prove it was Destiny that had sent Dominic out into the world and then led him to the pig's house and finally to the treasure, there was a piccolo, the very instrument he loved to play, made of solid gold.

He tested this new instrument immediately. The notes were golden, like the instrument itself. The gems flashing in the sunlight, the joyful music pouring from his piccolo, and the wild flowers all around him swept away the remnants of his gloom.

He was lost in delight. He was unaware that he'd

been encircled by a host of hostile beings. All the members of the Doomsday Gang—four foxes, three weasels, eight ferrets, a wildcat, a wolf, six tomcats, two dingoes, and a parcel of rats—armed to the teeth with various weapons, had formed a big ring around him, and were staring both at him and at the fabulous treasure from behind rocks, trees, hillocks, the house, the shed, the other outbuildings, and anything else that could hide them.

Suddenly Dominic's nose, which had been acting absent-minded, came to attention. It told him there was trouble brewing. He stopped playing, looked, and saw enough to know he was surrounded. His

spear! Where was his wonderful spear? He barked fiercely to intimidate his foes, raced to the house, seized his spear, and dashed back to the treasure before the mob of villains could reach it. Then they closed in.

What a battle royal raged! One, Dominic, against ever so many, the entire Doomsday Gang. They tried to grab any part of the treasure they could, they tried to subdue Dominic. But he was not to be bested, not to be subdued. It wasn't that he cared that much for treasure. He hated any kind of villainy. The villains wielded their weapons, swung their daggers, clubs, and swords; they attacked from the side, rushed in from the rear as well as from the front, but Dominic handled his wild spear with such swiftness, such force and ferocity, such cunning, that no scoundrel managed to touch the treasure.

Such a clashing and flashing of weapons in the sun's brightness! Never had anyone fought so furiously, so

fastidiously as Dominic did to protect the pig's precious jewels and his own precious self. This band of noxious nobodies had made the good pig miserable with their sneaky ways, and he was determined that not one of them should get a single pearl. Nor did it take the hole he had just dug to make him remember the hole they once thought they had him cornered in.

The battle went on and on and on and finally Dominic began to weary. So many against one. The villains could rest, could get a second wind, one, two, three at a time, but Dominic had no rest at all. He was panting furiously. He knew his strength couldn't last much longer; he would have to abandon the treasure and run, if he wanted to go on living. He looked around for a way out. There was none.

Then he heard something. Dimly at first, then rapidly getting louder, there was a most remarkable buzzing. The air was filled with the humming din of

thousands of angry yellow jackets, who swarmed from all points of the compass and funnelled in on the members of the Doomsday Gang, stinging right and left and in-between. What a howling and a yowling erupted! What a caterwauling! What shrieks, yelps, screams! What running and tumbling, what diving into ditches, what scrambling to hide—in deep grass, among trees and bushes, even in brambles.

The horde of avenging wasps drove the defeated Doomsday devils all over the summer landscape, and out of sight. It was a rout. But one wasp remained, and before he took off after the others, he made sure he had Dominic's attention, and described these words in the air:

Remember me?

"Thank you!" yelled Dominic.

Thank you

wrote the wasp.

VIII.

Dominic was exhausted. He looked lovingly at the departing yellow jacket, and dropped to the ground, where he rolled around in the cool grass until his panting subsided. Then he fell asleep and didn't wake up until morning, except once, briefly, to listen to an owl. "Why are there owls?" he asked himself. "Why anything?" he answered. And he was asleep again.

In the morning Dominic remembered something he had forgotten to do the day before, to make a proper, lasting headstone for Mr. Badger's grave. He found a flat piece of granite and chiselled out:

HERE LIES
BARTH. BADGER
A WONDERFUL PIG
HE LIVED ONE CENTURY

He fixed the stone at the head of the grave and firmed the earth around it. He laid some red roses at the foot of the grave. Again he had to cry. Then he went inside the house, ate breakfast, and packed some sandwiches, cookies, and fruit in his bandanna. After he'd locked up the house, he put the key back under the flowerpot at the left side of the door. He didn't know what else to do with it. He fastened the treasure

chests, closed the sack of gold coins, put the golden piccolo in his bandanna, and with some rope he found in the shed he somehow managed to tie the two chests and the sack on to his back. Then he said a silent goodbye to Mr. Badger and to his house, and staggered forth loaded down with tremendous wealth.

The weather was hot, and he was overburdened. He had to rest often. Late in the morning he stopped

by a happy waterfall and swam in the beautiful pool under it, enjoying the fluid feeling of union with the cool liquid. Afterwards he washed his clothes, hung them on his spear, and took a nap while they dried.

Well refreshed, he shouldered his burden again and went his way. But soon his legs began to weaken and wobble, and he wished that wealth didn't weigh so much. Now he had to go uphill and it felt even worse.

At the top of the hill he came upon a sleeping jackass. Dominic put down the load, twisting to lower it, and tapped him respectfully on the shoulder. No response. Dominic barked. This made the jackass jump, and then he was awake, or partially so. He succeeded in focusing on Dominic with bleary eyes. "Yes, what is it?" he asked, yawning.

"Good day," said Dominic. "I hope you're awake. I have a proposition to make to you. Do you see that baggage?" The jackass focused his tired eyes on the chests. "That baggage is full of treasure—pearls, gold, and precious stones. By the way, my name is Dominic. What's yours?"

"Elijah. Elijah Hogg," said the jackass. "How do you do?"

"The weight of those chests," said Dominic, getting to the point, "is too much for me. I'm not enjoying my travels. I'm tuckered out. I'll give you half of what's there if you'll carry my stuff. And me too."

"How far?" asked Elijah.

"How far?" Dominic repeated. "That's a good question. How far. How about our becoming companions and making it pretty far and quite a while?"

"Let's see the stuff," said the jackass.

Dominic opened the chests and the sack.

"It's a deal," said the jackass, too confounded to say any more.

The agreement settled, Dominic ate a sandwich while Elijah browsed in the clover. Then Dominic lashed his baggage on to the jackass, and with a running leap took a seat in front of it. They started down the other side of the hill.

"How much easier," thought Dominic, "to ride than to walk. What luxury! I do nothing and yet I'm moving forward, getting somewhere, and my baggage with me." Dominic was not at all lazy, far from it, but he'd worn himself out carrying so many times his own weight.

"Tell me, Elijah," he said, "have you ever run into the Doomsday bunch?"

"Have I ever? I certainly have," said Elijah. "They tried to get me to join their gang. And guess why! So they could ride me all over the countryside doing their wicked deeds. But I'm no fool, though I am a jackass. Since I refused to join up with them, they've given me quite a few unpleasant moments, I have scars here and there to show for it. And they've had quite a few kicks as souvenirs of yours truly."

Dominic, perched comfortably on Elijah's back, told about his own experiences with the gang. "You can expect to hear from them further," said Elijah. Sure enough, they soon came to a tree on which a sign was affixed with one spike. It carried a crude picture of Dominic and a message:

WANTED DEAD OR ALIVE
BY THE DOOMSDAY GANG
FOR TAKING TREASURE
WHICH WASN'T HIS.
DOMINIC, BEWARE!

Dominic, enraged, tore the sign down. Elijah trampled it into the ground with his hard hoofs. "They're not going to get *our* wealth!" he said.

They were in hilly country now. As they wove along

their way, Elijah groaned over the steepness of the rises. Even the downgrades were difficult, because he had to walk in awkward positions, his rear legs bent, his front ones straight. "My, this load is heavy," he kept saying. After a while he was groaning even on the level stretches. Dominic added to his discomfort by constant, restless fidgeting.

"Dominic," said Elijah, "let's make a new bargain. Give me less of the wealth. Deduct the part I get for carrying you, and get off my back."

Dominic jumped off. "As you like," he said. He was really happy to be on the ground again after his long rest and he romped around at Elijah's feet, tearing about with abandon, this way and that.

Soon they came to a field of alfalfa. Elijah loped straight into it and with all the baggage on his back began eating. "You know, Dominic," he said, "I'm a lazy jackass, I have to admit it. I wasn't meant to carry loads. And I don't really want to be rich. My, this is sweet alfalfa! How about taking the stuff off my back and calling off our agreement?"

Dominic understood. He didn't like carrying things either. "Sure, Elijah," he said, "if that's what you'd like." He rummaged in a chest, selected two of his best diamond necklaces, and hung one on each of Elijah's ears, where they seemed to belong. Then he shouldered the baggage, wished good cess to the wise jackass, and went on down the road.

Adorned with diamonds, Elijah grazed. He intended to live near that field of alfalfa for as many days as it took him to eat it, not rushing to finish, and indulging in all the daydreaming and stargazing that such work required.

IX. Again Dominic tired after a short trudge under his treasure, so he unburdened himself and lay down to rest. First he lay on his side, then on his back, where all he could see was the sky and his own paws, then on his belly with his face in the cool grass. In a moment he was all astonished eyes and perked-up ears. A stone right in front of him had put out a head! Dominic pulled himself together. "Good day to you, sir," he said respectfully.

"Good day," said the turtle. "That's some heap of appurtenances you've got there."

Dominic rolled over on his back and put his paws behind his head. He said, "I'll bet you can't guess what's in those chests."

"Your things," said the turtle.

"Yes, they're my things all right," said Dominic. "But what are they?"

"Clothes, pots, dishes, bric-a-brac, stuff like that."

"Guess again."

"Merchandise to sell at the market," said the turtle. "Picture hooks, carpet tacks, embroidery frames, and darning needles."

"Nope," said Dominic, smiling. "Guess again."

"The tools of your trade," said the turtle. "Brushes and pots if you're a painter; hammers, nails, pliers, screwdrivers, if you're a carpenter . . ."

"Guess once more," said Dominic.

"I know," said the turtle, laughing. "You're the Sultan of Shizzam, the richest sovereign in the universe, and those chests are crammed to the brim with gold and diamonds!"

It was Dominic's turn to laugh. He flung open both chests, and the turtle, expecting to see something commonplace, or perhaps just a little out of the ordinary, almost flipped over backward. Now, realizing how wrong he had been when he thought he was right and how right he had been when he thought he was wrong, he really rocked with laughter, shaking inside his shell, while Dominic stood there with a look of pride and satisfaction, his seaman's hat tilted over one ear.

"Heavens! However did you come by all this?" the turtle finally asked.

Dominic sat down, sighed, and told him the whole story, including the episodes involving the Doomsday Gang.

"I know *them*," said the turtle. "Everybody hereabouts knows them. But they're no problem for me. They turn up, I go into my shell. They can rap on it all they want, I don't pay attention. Flip me over, I just lie on my back. After a while they get fed up with nothing happening and leave. Sooner or later help comes along and I get straightened out and go on about my business. Too bad you don't have a shell like me."

Dominic didn't understand the turtle's point of view. If he had a shell, he wouldn't hide in it. Whenever there was trouble, his philosophy was to go right out and meet it at least halfway. And he was surprised that anyone should react otherwise. He decided to introduce himself. "My name is Dominic, what's yours?"

"Lemuel Wallaby. Funny name for a turtle, isn't it. It goes back in my family many generations, and each generation is a hundred years."

"And how old are you?" asked Dominic.

"Two hundred and fifty-eight."

"Wow!" said Dominic. "Wow, wow! That's pretty old."

"Not for a turtle." The truth is that Lemuel was only *one* hundred and fifty-eight; it was his habit to exaggerate his age in order to make an impression.

Since Dominic was just a year and a half old and felt quite mature, it was not easy for him to think of any age much beyond that as young. "I have a proposition to make you," he said, changing the subject. "How would you like to be a wealthy turtle? A very wealthy turtle? All you have to do is carry the treasure for me and I'll share it with you fifty-fifty."

"How far?" asked Lemuel.

"Reasonably far," said Dominic. "And if you like my company, you can continue after that."

"It's a deal," said the turtle. "Let's go."

Dominic strapped the chests and the sack on to the turtle's back and they started out side by side. But after only a few seconds Dominic was way down the road and the turtle had barely moved. Dominic came running back.

"Anything wrong?" he asked.

"Nope," answered Lemuel.

"Let's go faster then," said Dominic.

"This is my usual speed," said Lemuel. "Perhaps the weight slows me down a trifle. I'm not sure. I'll have to think it over. I usually make half a mile in a day of travelling."

Dominic could make a mile in two minutes. "No wonder you live so long," he said. "If you didn't, you'd never get anywhere." He tried tiptoeing alongside the turtle but he couldn't tiptoe slowly enough. He decided to explore the surrounding countryside while Lemuel inched his way along the road. He discovered a wonderful waterfall and was in and out

of it six times. He met some horses mowing a field
of grass. He watched them work and he talked with
them on any number of subjects, including the
weather and the diet of vegetarians. And when he
ran back to the road, Lemuel didn't seem to have
advanced any.

"You know," said Lemuel, "the weight *might* be
slowing me down. It's not really too slow for *me*,
but I can tell it's too slow for you. You're a bit high-
strung. Anyway, I have an idea. Tie the stuff to your
back. Then get on my back. That will make it easier
for both of us. You'll be carrying the stuff, but resting, and I'll only be carrying you."

Dominic was willing to try that, and they did, but Lemuel said it was worse, which of course it was, and Dominic got impatient just sitting and moving

along at so painful a pace. It was not like riding on Elijah Hogg. It exasperated him, threatened to sour his good humour.

He finally blurted out, "I can't stand this, Lemuel. I know you're a fine young athletic turtle. Perhaps you're the fastest turtle in this part of the world, but your pace is killing me. The whole arrangement isn't working out as I expected. Do you mind if we undo our agreement?"

Lemuel didn't mind, because he wasn't too crazy

about walking, especially with a heavy load on his back. Sometimes he spent entire days just standing in one place, not even thinking about anything, not even wondering, just being there.

Dominic gave Lemuel a few gold pieces and a ruby ring, which the turtle stashed away somewhere inside his shell. Then he kissed Lemuel goodbye on top of his bony head, shouldered his load, and streaked off. He felt frantic with freedom after the turtle's impossible slowness. The weight seemed like nothing, a pack of fluff, sacks of air.

After a while, of course, he felt the heaviness again. And that night he slept like a log—a soft, sighing log.

X. Dominic woke in the morning, a blissful smile on his face. The gentle radiance of a rosy sun pervaded the air, and little birds sang so lyrically that he took out his golden piccolo and joined them in their music. The world was suffused with peace and warmth. Dominic danced through the grass. Then, overcome with exultation, he flung his spear high in the air, where the early sun painted it pink for a moment.

He ate the last of his cookies for breakfast, washed himself by rolling in the dew, and was off once more with his load on his back.

Very soon he came upon a wild boar weeping. "Why are you weeping?" asked Dominic.

"Oh, I have such bad luck, such bad luck," moaned the miserable boar. "It's a long story."

"Tell it," said Dominic.

"Well, to be brief," said the boar, "I'm in love. Never have I been so much in love. Oh, she's wonderful! Such bristles. Such snow-white teeth. Such warm brown eyes. Such grace when she moves. Well, not to go on too much about it, we're to be married. That is, we *were* to be married. Now, I don't know.

"For two years I've been saving up for a wedding and a honeymoon, and to build a house to live in. We'd decided to stop being wild and become civilized. Oh, how happy we were, planning our future. Just one week from today the wedding was to take place. I had all the money hidden in a cave, where I was sure no one could find it. No one else knew about it—so I thought.

"This morning I went to count the money. Do you like to count money? I . . ." At this point, overcome with sorrow and bitterness, the boar began weeping again. He had to strike the ground over and over to vent his feelings. Dominic felt so sorry for him, he had to cry too.

In a while the boar was able to continue. "To get on with my story, I went to count the money. I sat with it in front of me, dreaming of my loved one and the charming house we would live in. A house near a brook, with a pretty garden, a bird bath . . . Do you love birds?" Dominic nodded. "It was to have a billiard table in the rumpus room, by the way. I love billiards . . . Well, as I was saying . . . What was I saying? Oh, yes. Suddenly I was surrounded by that Doomsday Gang. They jumped me and began beat-

ing me with sticks and stones. I fought like a tiger. But they were too many. They tied me up and made off with my money.

"It took me two hours to chew through the ropes. I started out to find my fiancée but I broke down crying here on the road where you met me." Another sob escaped the boar, just one. He restrained himself.

Dominic was overwhelmed with indignation at the hoodlums and flooded with compassion for the hapless boar. He said, "I think Fate has sent me your way. You can have your wedding, and your honeymoon and your house and furniture as well, and still have a little left over for any possible emergency."

And in an upsurge of bountiful feeling, he emptied both chests on the grass and heaped part of their contents before the boar, whose mouth fell open, revealing the full length of his tusks. Dominic fished some gold out of the sack and dropped that on the pile.

The boar couldn't speak. Now Dominic picked out a beautiful nose ring of emeralds and amethysts, and said, "How about this trinket as a wedding ring for your bride?"

The boar began crying again. Not out of sorrow this time, but out of excruciating joy. "How can I ever, ever in this world, not to mention the next, and disregardless of unforeseen contingencies, adequately thank you!" he said. "I can't even begin, let alone work up a proper preamble to a beginning, to tell you how unendurably happy you've made me. But I'll try . . ."

"Never mind," said Dominic, "I know how you feel." He was beginning to think it took the boar too long to say whatever he had to say.

"You must come to my wedding," said the boar. "Remember, one week from today. Ask for Barney Swain—that's my name. Everyone around here knows me and will know about the wedding."

"My name is Dominic," said Dominic. "I'll surely come if I'm in the neighbourhood."

He had given the boar so much of the treasure, it filled one of the chests. They scooped up the gems, the gold, and the pearls that remained on the grass and carefully packed them in the other chest. While this was going on, the little beady eyes of two rats out scouting for the Doomsday Gang were watching from behind the bushes. Dominic didn't smell them because the wind was blowing the wrong way.

XI.

Dominic and Barney Swain said goodbye. The boar went off with the chest on his shoulder to break the news to his bride-to-be, both the good news that was embodied in Dominic's gift, and the bad news, about the Doomsday Gang having taken his money, which was no longer such bad news on account of the good news. He thought he would tell her the bad news first so the good news when he got to it would make her that much happier. But actually he didn't want to make her feel unhappy even for a little while. So he decided he would just open the chest, show her what was in it, and then explain everything as best he could, trying to make a long story short.

And Dominic fared forth on his own way with a much springier step, because he had one less chest to carry. Where was he going? He didn't really know, but he looked forward to finding out.

Around a bend in the road he came across an animal lying on the ground, tearing at his own fur and crying his heart out. The animal was wearing dark glasses, a broad-brimmed hat, and a cape that came down to his heels.

"Why are you crying?" asked Dominic, pretending to be taken in. He knew who was hiding under those clothes.

"Oh, pity me," said the animal. "Pity me. You see before you one of the most miserable and unfortunate wretches that ever existed on this planet. This morning, this very, very morning, a lovely morning as you may remember, I was as rich as anyone would want to be, but now I'm a pauper. And I was to be married very, very soon to one of the most lovely fe-

males in creation. But that Doomsday Gang—surely you've heard of them—purloined my money."

Dominic was not fooled by this story. The speaker wearing the disguise was the fox, who had forgotten to consider that wise and sensitive instrument, Dominic's all-knowing nose. Dominic would have recognized his smell merely by sniffing something he had touched only lightly a year earlier. How could he fail to smell the fox himself, the very fox who had had him down in the hole, who had attacked him after he buried Mr. Badger?

"Oh, you poor creature," said Dominic, as he put down his load and removed the bandanna he carried on his spear. "You poor, unhappy, ill-treated, miserable . . . mean, cruel, scheming, criminal of a fox! Say your prayers, you scoundrel, for you're about to get what's due you. I have a debt I long to pay."

The villainous fox was unarmed, and he knew about Dominic's spear and the way he wielded it. Yelping with fear, he was off like an arrow from a bow, Dominic right after him, spear levelled.

But the fox got away. Dominic didn't chase him too far, fearing that some other member, or members, of the gang might steal the treasure left unguarded. He came back and studiously sniffed the air, making certain that no one was around except the insects and birds that belonged there. Then he started on his way again.

The road now ran alongside a gully, where Dominic discovered the rib cage of a large animal that had perished there quite some time ago. It was like a feast laid out for him, and he was ravenous. Despite their age, the ribs tasted good. In fact, age had added a rich, musty tang which only a connoisseur of bones could properly appreciate. Dominic gnawed rapturously.

While the savoury bones were receiving his total attention, the fox he had recently routed, along with two more members of the Doomsday Gang, another fox and a ferret, was sneaking up to attack him from behind. Dominic was inside the rib cage, in a sort of succulent prison, and they might have trapped him there; but when they saw him chewing on the big bones with such furious dedication, they were paralyzed with terror. "That dog," the ferret managed to whisper from his dry throat, "is a mighty fearsome creature to have killed so enormous an animal!"

"Yes," said the fox, "and he may still be hungry. I didn't realize what we were dealing with. It will take more than three of us to subdue him."

"You said it," said the second fox. "You certainly said it!" And they tiptoed off, cautious not to crackle a dry twig, or kick a single pebble, or make any sound that would distract Dominic from the bones.

XII.

When Dominic had eaten his fill, he lay down. Just a few scratches, a dozen yawns, a short snooze, and he was on his way again.

He soon passed a big stand of pine trees. Their special spicy scent was a tonic. High up on a hickory not far ahead of him, he was startled to see a goose hanging by the feet, and he hurried towards her.

Standing on the treasure chest, he used his spear to cut the rope and get the goose down. "Mercy me!" she cried. "There's smelling salts in my reticule . . ." And fluttering her wings, she fainted. Dominic managed to bring her to with the smelling salts. She looked around with addled eyes.

"Dear dog, dear darling dog," she exclaimed. "I thought my life was over! Imagine! To be hanged, to be hanged by the feet while on the way to market! And me a widow with children to look after!"

"What happened?" asked Dominic.

"I was on my way to market," she said tremulously. "So many things we need at home. Soap, flour, sugar. My tea is practically gone, just a few leaves left in the bottom of the canister. I thought I'd get some cookies for the children—chocolate chip or coconut—some gooseberry jam, some oranges . . . But these four—I think it was four—these four masked ruffians came pouring out of the trees, and the first thing I knew, I was hanging where you found me. I heard one of them say, 'We'll roast her tonight, after we find the cranberries,' and then they were gone. Roast, indeed! I wonder how *they* would like to be roasted—with or without cranberries. As if I didn't have other plans for my life! I don't know how long I've been hanging there. I fainted and came to several times. I thought of the joys of swimming, flying, walking, with my little ones. I felt how I loved them and how much they needed me, and I didn't want to die. Goodness! If you hadn't come by when you did, there'd be one less goose in the world! How can I ever repay you?"

"Your life is my reward," said Dominic, bowing. "With you in the world, the world is a better place, I'm sure. My name is Dominic. And I am at your service, madam." Dominic was exceptionally attentive to ladies.

The goose, getting into the spirit of things, gracefully curtsied. "My name," she said, "is Matilda Fox.

I live hereabouts. In case you're interested in how a goose got the name Fox, I had an extremely intelligent ancestor. He was so smart they called him The Fox. Eventually the name was entered in the Hall of Records, and became the surname of our family. I think one of my sons takes after him."

"How interesting," said Dominic politely. "May I take you home?"

"I'd be delighted," said the goose. "This is the way." She took up her reticule and shopping basket, Dominic took up his load, and they set off, waddling and walking down the road.

Soon they came to the goose's cottage, situated by a pond in a secluded spot. Five goslings were swim-

ming in the pond, chattering back and forth and making a ruckus, as children often do. Mrs. Fox called them to the bank and introduced them one by one. Their names were Alpha, Beta, Gamma, Delta, and Epsilon.

Dominic was enchanted with them. He had tender feelings for young ones of any sort, even for the babies of snakes, a species he otherwise regarded with disfavour.

Dominic praised Mrs. Fox's home and her family and she urged him to stay on as long as he liked. He stayed. He frolicked with the children, and had diverting and informative conversations with their mother. The children liked to hear him play his piccolo, especially while they swam. They would sometimes do a sort of water dance, a liquid minuet, to his music. In a water-polo game one day, the goslings played rings around him, and Dominic was abashed at being bested by such small creatures. But he said to himself: "If water polo was played on land, I could beat them."

Mrs. Fox fattened Dominic up with all sorts of elegant cookery—delicious soups, fragrant salads, heavenly pastries, and a variety of dishes made with rare herbs and subtle sauces. He enjoyed sniffing out the ingredients, "guessing" what was in her recipes, and of course he was always right.

After these wonderful meals, he would lie dreaming in the hammock, or he'd sit by the pond with Mrs. Fox, watching the children and conversing. They spoke of many things. Mrs. Fox spoke of her dead husband, who apparently had been an excep-

tional goose, and of the problems of raising children without a father. Dominic spoke of his home, his friends, and his thirst for adventure and knowledge of life. Once he asked Mrs. Fox which she liked to do best, walk, swim, or fly; and this was her answer:

"I know most creatures can't do all three, and I hope you'll pardon me for saying that I can't understand how they manage that way. Personally, I wouldn't want to give up any means of locomotion—in the air, on water, or on land. All three are necessary. Since I spend most of my time on land, naturally I have to be able to walk. It wouldn't make much sense flying between the icebox and the sink, and swimming is useless where there's no water. Walking is good for thinking. And different kinds of walking are good for different kinds of thinking. For

example, walking back and forth in a small space is good for thinking about your worries. At times, walking is hard on the feet. Certain kinds of gravel really hurt the webbing between my toes, and there are places I have to avoid for that reason. I love to play tennis, which of course you must do on your feet. I love to work in my garden, pick flowers, and do many other things which can only be done on land.

"Water feels good, even when it's cold, and swimming, as you know, is a great pleasure. It's a handy way to cross a stream when there's no bridge. Flying is another way, but of course I can't fly when I'm loaded down with things, which I often am—my reticule, my umbrella, my shopping basket, books from the library, et cetera. I couldn't get off the ground."

"Of course not," said Dominic understandingly.

Mrs. Fox continued: "Swimming is not as good for thinking as walking is, but swimming is wonderful for woolgathering. I love to float with the current of the stream, listen to the gentle lapping by the shore line, and dream whatever daydreams want to be dreamed. It's so peaceful. Whenever I feel nerveracked, worrying too much about things, getting depressed or irritable, wherever I am, I look for water and go for a swim. It's balm. It's like being back in the egg, floating without a care in benign albumen. And of course it's cleansing. Now as to flying, that's a hard thing to describe to someone without wings."

"I sometimes dream I'm flying," Dominic volunteered.

"Flying is pure delight," said Mrs. Fox, "unless you are being chased by birds of prey. There's a rhythm to flying and it's the rhythm of the universe.

It's a cosmic experience. Up there, and especially high up, I feel close to my Maker—I have the conviction that life is eternal and I will see my dead husband again, rest his soul. Floating on air currents, rising with the updrafts of warm air, sliding on the downdrops, I feel in perfect harmony with natural events. I feel athletic, graceful. Flying is, of course, the quickest and straightest way from point A to point B, no obstruction to be moved around, over or under. It's the best way for travelling south in winter and north in the spring. And it's ideal for getting a broad view of things. Well, to answer your original question, it would be hard to say which I like best. Each is best in its own way."

Dominic understood and had to agree, though he could not swim as well as a goose and could fly only in his dreams.

By and by, at the end of three days to be exact, he grew restless, anxious to pursue his journey and meet his future. Before leaving, he built a high fence of strong metal netting around the Fox property and strung barbed wire on top of it. And after careful consideration, he filled his pockets with gold pieces and selected a ring to keep for himself. Then he put a pearl necklace around the neck of each gosling, at which they honked their delight, and gave all the rest of the treasure to Mrs. Fox.

"I can't possibly accept such largess," she protested. "You are too good. It is I who am indebted to you.

You saved my life. Think what would have happened to my children without me."

She would have gone on, but Dominic stopped her. "Madam," he said, "Matilda—if I may call you by your first name—I have spent a few of the happiest days of my life in your little Garden of Eden. I have enjoyed your children. Conversation with you has broadened my horizons. I am in the best possible health as a result of your good care. Furthermore, I really have no use for wealth. I'm young, I'm free, and I have a God-given nose to guide me through life. Please, say no more."

Overwhelmed by his own generosity and the sadness of parting, he kissed each darling gosling with a tear in his eye, hugged and kissed Mrs. Fox, and was off into the world without further ado.

A moment later Mrs. Fox came flying after him

with some pastries to put in his bandanna and they had to say goodbye again.

Striding along, aglow with the energy he had stored up resting and feeding so well, he felt marvellously carefree. He had brought great good fortune and happiness to the Foxes, and had earned their gratitude, at the same time ridding himself of an encumbrance.

XIII. Dominic was so happy he whipped out his piccolo and played, allegro tempo. How lovely everything looked! He was filled with adoration for the visible world. Ah, what splendid red roses there on that bush in the road. He sniffed at them eagerly, but smelled nothing, and—thump!—he bumped into a painting.

The artist, a wee mouse, was rolling on the ground laughing. Dominic sat up and touched the painting. He felt he could pick a rose off the bush, and yet it was nothing but paint and canvas. He looked at the mouse in wonder. The little creator had cobalt blue on his moustache, cadmium yellow on his foot, and thalo green on the seat of his overalls.

"Did you paint this?" Dominic asked.

"Yes," said the mouse with obvious pride.

"You're a clever artist," said Dominic. "I was really fooled. But why is your painting standing here in the road?"

"Allow me to introduce myself," said the mouse. "My name is Manfred Lyon. Fine name for a mouse, isn't it!"

"I'm Dominic," said Dominic. They shook paws and Dominic enjoyed the delicacy of Manfred Lyon's touch.

"To answer your question," the mouse went on, "I love to paint, and I love to paint in this *trompe l'oeil* style. Everything is so beautiful just as it is that I pay my respects to life by painting things just as they are.

Some of my brushes have but a single hair in them, which I get from my own eyebrows, and with my sharp eyes I can see and paint the finest details: every vein in every leaf, the highlight on a drop of dew, the hair on the legs of a gnat. I know the work of a very great artist, an elephant. He can't paint detail. He has neither the ability nor the patience. In any case . . . I put my painting in the road just now to test its verisimilitude, to assure myself that my skill is as great as I suspect it is."

"I assure you that it is," said Dominic. "I'll admit my eyesight is not as keen as my sense of smell—what is? Still, I've never been fooled by a painting before. If one goes by that sort of standard, you are as fine an artist as ever lived." Dominic could hardly believe such highfalutin talk was coming out of his own yap. When he got over being impressed with himself, he continued. "But everywhere I look, I see beauty. If I can see a lovely landscape, just as lovely as one painted by Manfred Lyon, only by looking out my window, why would I want to own a painting done in that style? It's the same as what I can see wherever I turn."

"I've considered that," said the mouse, "and this is my answer: When the landscape is covered with snow, can you see leaves? In the midst of a dreary winter, when you are longing for spring, you can look at the daffodils in a painting of mine and be confident that there *is* such a season as spring and

that it will come again. When you are suffering in excessive summer heat, you can encourage yourself by looking at a cold winter landscape painted by Manfred Lyon. You can keep in a sort of contact with an absent friend or loved one through a portrait by me. Anyway . . . I dislike theorizing. I'd rather paint than think. Painting is fun, but thinking hurts my brains." He scratched the base of his tail, depositing a touch of vermilion there.

"I get the point," said Dominic. "Thank you for explaining."

"Do you mind helping me straighten up my painting?" said the mouse. "I use those ropes hanging from that pulley," and he pointed to the limb of a tree overhead. Dominic pushed the painting into its original, upright position without the help of the

ropes, and propped it up from behind with some sticks the mouse pointed out.

"Well, back to the old drawing board," he joked, picking up his tiny brushes.

Dominic laughed. "I think I'll be hitting the road," he said. "So long." And he was off with his lance on his shoulder, his bandanna swinging from it, and gold jingling in his pocket.

"How did the world ever manage without me before I was born?" he wondered. "Didn't they feel something was missing?"

A little farther down the road, he was accosted by a large group of rabbits. There they were, standing in the road, obviously waiting for this particular individual, him, Dominic, to turn up, and they were not a painting.

The one who was to be their spokesman was too shy for the part. He had to be pushed by the others and stood timidly in front, his moustache trembling. Dominic, with customary directness, rushed right up to the group. That didn't help. The spokesman lost the power of speech.

"Greetings," said Dominic. "You are obviously waiting for me and wish to say something."

This loosened the rabbit's tongue. "Oh, yes," he said. "I would like to make a statement."

"Then speak," said Dominic.

"You're Dominic," said the rabbit. "Your reputation is spreading hereabouts. Everyone knows how you've been tangling with the Doomsday hooligans, and getting the best of them. We all know about your courage and your powerful lance. Those villains have been terrorizing us—we fear for our lives and worry about our property. They despise us so much they've assigned just a weasel and a stoat to plague us. And those two manage very well. We need protection and would like you to be our protector. We can pay."

Dominic was touched and also flattered at this expression of confidence in his prowess. But the rabbits' fearfulness made him uncomfortable. In a way, he respected the members of the Doomsday Gang more than he respected the rabbits. The Doomsday Gang were sometimes cowards too, but they also had plenty of nerve. He found himself telling a lie almost against his will: "I'm sorry, but much as I'd like to help you,

I'm already late for an appointment ten miles away."

The rabbits looked so disappointed that Dominic felt a twinge of reluctant compassion. "I have an idea," he said. And he told them about Manfred Lyon, the artist he had just met down the road. "Get Mr. Lyon to paint a picture of some of you browsing in clover. Set traps in front of the picture and then hide somewhere. If Manfred Lyon's painting can fool me, it will fool your weasel and stoat. And when you have them in the traps, you can dispose of them as you please. I'm sorry I can't stay to see the results. I must really be on my way. Good day to you all."

"Won't you please reconsider?" asked the spokesman.

"No."

"We'd pay you well," said another rabbit.

"I'm sorry," said Dominic.

"Then I guess we'll try your plan," said the spokesman. "Thank you ever so much for the suggestion."

"Not at all." And Dominic went on his way without waiting to see if his plan worked. Here, briefly, is what happened:

The rabbits, who already knew Manfred Lyon, found him quickly and offered him a large sum of money, plus two sacks of carrots, to paint the picture as Dominic described it. Money or no, the artist was only too happy for a chance to test his skill in this interesting way, and to see the villains suffer as a result. After making sketches of several rabbits, he painted the picture in a few days, working at night too, by the light of a kerosene lamp and candles.

The weasel and the stoat were thoroughly deceived by the picture. Creeping up on the painted rabbits

eating their painted clover, they somehow failed to notice that the rabbits didn't move, perhaps because they were so intent on what appeared to be an easy success.

There were enough traps to catch dozens of victims, so inevitably they were caught. The rabbits, in large numbers, bound the weasel and the stoat in chains before releasing them from the traps, and carried them to a granary they had converted into a prison while the mouse was painting.

Timid creatures incapable of cruelty, the rabbits

were unable to inflict punishment. They planned to rehabilitate the stoat and the weasel, to teach them the unwisdom of evil and gradually to inculcate into them sentiments of pity, mercy, charity, and love. And they told them so. It might have worked, but the stoat and the weasel were not interested in learning this new point of view. They thought such decency was based only on fear, and as soon as the sun went down and the rabbits had finished lecturing and left them alone, they picked the locks and made their escape. Not many days afterward, they got their just deserts.

Manfred Lyon was disappointed to hear of the prison break, but he was satisfied that his painting had served the cause of justice, and he felt free to boast about it now and then.

XIV.

By the time the unrepentant criminals had made their escape, Dominic was much farther along his way, nothing special having happened to him meanwhile.

It was a moonlight night. All moonlight is magical and puts us under a spell, but some moonlight nights move our tides more than others and even make us a little bit daffy. This was such a night. It was out of the question for Dominic to go to sleep, though it was his usual hour for retiring. He wasn't tired. The night and everything under its influence was alive, awake, and spellbound. Fireflies flickered high and low. It was not clear where the fireflies ended and the stars began.

Dominic wandered into a field where he saw what appeared to be miniature Japanese lanterns. They *were* miniature Japanese lanterns. Mice were having a moonlight revel in a clearing surrounded by tall grass and they had strung their prismatic lanterns between stalks of timothy. Dominic, enchanted, watched the proceedings from the top of a rock. There was delicate, stately mouse music produced by tiny zithers, lutes, and tambourines. Dominic took out his piccolo and played, softly, ever so softly. The mice heard but didn't question where the piccolo notes were coming from. They too were bewitched.

They danced cotillions and polkas. Some of the ladies wore elegant gowns, and feathers to adorn their lovely heads. Their jewellery, gems no bigger than

poppy seeds, sparkled in the moonlight. Many of the men were tipsy on oko, a beverage made from fermented honey and acorns. The revelry grew more and more ecstatic, the music strove nearer and nearer to the elemental truth of being.

All this and the moon was too much for Dominic's overflowing soul. He couldn't help himself. He raised his head and, straining toward infinity, howled out the burden of his love and longing in sounds more meaningful than words. This unexpected outburst broke the spell for the mice, and they fled in terror, leaving an empty place lighted by the moon and the tiny lanterns.

Dominic was sorry he had ended the celebration. He walked in the field smelling daisies, marigolds, black-eyed Susans, and sweet grass. He found a doll lying in the grass and he gathered from its appearance that it had been lost some time ago. It was a likable doll, a long-eared puppy with shoe-button eyes, one of them hanging by a thread from its socket.

The smell of the doll intrigued him. It had the same magical effect as the moonlight. It inspired a longing. For what? He wasn't sure. He tenderly tucked the doll away in his bandanna and continued to wander about in the field.

Finally he was moved to look to the heavens and declare: "Oh, Life, I am yours. Whatever it is you want of me, I am ready to give." And again he couldn't help howling. He howled and he howled,

without restraint, embarrassment, or self-conscious-
ness. These howls had been gathering in him for a
long time and it was wonderful release to vent them
in their fullness.

He strayed farther into the meadow. And sure
enough, considering the hypnotic quality of the
moon, there was a somnambulist abroad—a sleepwalking goat in nightcap and nightshirt roaming this way
and that, forelegs extended, feeling his way through
space. Dominic had heard somewhere that you mustn't
waken a sleepwalker unless the situation demands it:
unless he is about to walk out of an open window, or

into a deep pond or the fireplace, or over broken glass or whatever.

So he walked quietly alongside the goat and they moved into grass over Dominic's ears, disturbing two hedgehogs who had been trysting in the moonlight and who made outcries of indignation; and then they went up a small hill and over a knoll and into a wood —the goat all the while holding his own dreamy counsel—and through some underbrush and out again into an open field and then down a slope and then ankle deep into a cool rill and then over some rocks, and finally Dominic had had enough of traipsing alongside a somnambulist. He guided the goat into a tree that proved to be unyielding.

"Where am I?" said the goat, with the tree in his embrace. "What am I doing here?"

"You are on the planet Earth, embracing a tree in a field under the full moon," answered Dominic, "and it's as lovely a night as ever there was since time began."

"And who are you?" the goat inquired.

"My name is Dominic."

"Who am I?"

"I know this much," said Dominic. "My eyes, my ears, and my nose tell me you're a goat."

"Goat? Then I must be Phineas Matterhorn. I'm confused."

"You've been sleepwalking," said Dominic.

"Ah," said Phineas, "I *am* a sleepwalker, so it must

be me. I'm beginning to get my bearings now. Tell me this, am I headed in the direction of Grandville, where Barney Swain and Pearl Sweeney will be celebrating their wedding?"

"You've been walking in every possible direction— at times you must have been headed that way," said Dominic. "When is the wedding?"

"Tomorrow. I'm going. I dreamed I was already on my way."

"Let's go together," said Dominic. "I've been invited too."

"It will be a gala event," said Phineas. "I hear Barney came into a lot of money from some rich relative in the import-export business, and he's really splurging on this affair."

"You don't say!" said Dominic, musing on how news sometimes gets distorted.

"The Doomsdays tried to steal his money," the goat went on, "but he routed the whole gang single-handed."

"You don't say!" said Dominic. "You double don't say!"

"He bought his bride-to-be the most wonderful wedding ring for her nose, diamonds and amethysts in it the size of peas."

"Wow!" said Dominic. "Wow, wow, wow!" He was momentarily angry at the way the truth tends to change its shape and get more worn and more unrecognizable the more it's passed around.

"Ah well. Let's go," he said, and they set out, walking slowly, enjoying the lunar light, and chatting.

"Use your horns much?" asked Dominic. He tried to imagine having such protuberances on his own head, but it was difficult.

"I guess I do," said the goat. "I don't think about it. I'm not always conscious I have horns. But I sure remember them whenever I get into a physical debate with the Doomsdays."

Dominic smiled at the goat's odd way of putting things. "What do you like best about weddings?" he asked.

"I like it all," said Phineas. "The festive feeling, the food, the music, the dancing, the fancy clothing, the decorations, the gaiety. But I think I like best just being there among so many with so much going on—being seen, feeling central, and being admired by one and all, or imagining I'm being admired by one and all, which comes to the same thing. It doesn't matter that others feel *they* are the centre of attraction, *they* are the life of the party. I know *I* am, as they know *they* are, and everyone's happy and all is one. Which is why parties are so wonderful!"

As they talked, they approached a strange, bulky shape. It moved and they hurried toward it to see what it was, Dominic arriving first. It was a pygmy elephant sitting in the road. He was small even for a pygmy elephant; indeed, he wasn't much bigger than Dominic. Preoccupied with whatever was on his

mind, he didn't even notice the two curious animals standing at his side, casting their shadows over him.

"Begging your pardon, sir," said Dominic to the stranger. "I hope you are enjoying the beauty of this rare moonstruck night."

The pygmy elephant turned his head, startled. "Good evening," he said. "I'm in trouble."

"Can we help you?" asked Dominic.

"No, I don't think so. Maybe. Maybe you can. Let me introduce myself first. My name is Mwana Bhomba."

"Strange name," said Phineas Matterhorn.

"I come from Africa," said Mwana Bhomba.

"Oh," said the goat. "I'm Phineas Matterhorn and

this is my friend Dominic. What seems to be the trouble?"

"You probably won't believe me," said the elephant, "but I can do magic and thereby get anything I wish for. That is to say, I *could* do magic if I could only remember the magic word. If I ever remember the word, the first thing I'm going to do is wish I never forget it again."

"That's clever," said Dominic. "How did you get your magic?"

"You see," said the elephant, "a witch doctor, a crocodile witch doctor at home where I live, gave me this magic word. I don't know why. He said he was used to seeing big elephants and I was so little. He said a little elephant like me needed magic to make his way in the world. Well, he gave it to me. And the first thing I did was wish myself in some faraway place, any romantic faraway place, and here I am."

"This rare moon must have pulled you our way," Dominic decided.

"It's lovely here. You have a very nice country," said the elephant. "But I want to wish myself back home in Africa, and I can't, however I try, remember the magic word."

"What a pity!" said Dominic. "What does it sound like?"

"It sounds like Jest, I think, but I don't think it begins with J."

"What do you think it begins with?"

"A, F, G, P, or H. But I'm not sure it's any one of those. It could be an L." The elephant went on to say it could begin with any letter of the alphabet and that it was a really simple, very common word and maybe that's what made it hard to remember.

"Aren't elephants supposed to have good memories?" asked the goat.

"Yes," said Mwana Bhomba, "and that's why I didn't write the word down on a piece of paper, as I should have, or even better, have it tattooed on my leg. I committed it to memory, and my memory won't give it up."

"Well," said Dominic, pacing about, his paws behind his back. "What we have to do is go through all the words we know, and if it's a simple word, as you say, we'll get it sooner or later. It probably starts with some letter late in the alphabet, so let's not be fools and begin with A. Let's begin with Z and go backward. Is it Zylophone?"

"Xylophone starts with an X," said the goat.

"Is it Zebra?" asked Dominic.

"No," said the elephant.

"Is it Zero?"

"No."

"Zigzag?"

"No."

There were a few more Z's. "All right, Y," said the goat. "How about Yogurt?"

"No," said the elephant.

"How about Yearling. Yearning. Yesterday. Yak. Yellow. Yolk."

"No," said the elephant.

"Let's do this as we walk," said Dominic. "Come with us to the wedding of the boars, Barney and Pearl. They'll surely welcome any friend of ours. Somewhere along the line we'll discover your word, because we're proceeding in an intelligent manner and are therefore bound to meet with success. Cheer up! We'll find the magic word for you."

Heartened by these reassurances, the elephant got up off the ground and they walked along at a leisurely pace, testing various words. When they had gone through X, W, V, U, T, S, R, Q, and P, they arrived at a place where some odd goings-on were in progress. They were looking down into a dell, in which a woodchuck, a beaver, a raccoon, and a porcupine were performing a strange ritual.

The woodchuck, the beaver, the raccoon, and the porcupine salaamed to the moon, and salaamed to each other. Then they walked slowly in a circle, bowing to the north, to the east, to the south, and to the west. They then lay down on the ground and rolled three times clockwise and three times counter-clockwise. After that, the porcupine sprinkled the woodchuck, the raccoon, and the beaver with coconut oil. Next the raccoon threw sesame seeds at the porcu-

pine, the woodchuck, and the beaver. Whereupon the beaver read some words out of a big book and all four kissed the book. The woodchuck then put on a tall hat covered with emblems and touched each of the others with a willow wand. Once more, and solemnly, they walked around in a circle. It was very impressive and mysterious, and Dominic, Phineas, and Mwana never found out what it all meant, because the woodchuck, the beaver, the raccoon, and the porcupine belonged to a secret society that never let out its secrets. *They* knew what they were doing, just as you and I know what we're doing when we do the things we do, and that's all that matters.

Dominic, Phineas, and Mwana continued on their way to the wedding. "How about Olive?" asked Dominic. "Oriole. Oboe. Obelisk. Oomph. Overcoat. Ottoman. Orchids. Orchard. Open. Ocelot. Oodles. Oink. Ointment. Only."

"None of those," said Mwana. There was a dimming of the light. The moon had crossed most of the sky and was near the horizon, preparing to set.

"Oarlock. Obbligato. Octet. October. Odour. Onyx. Opossum. Oxygen. Oak," said Phineas. The elephant looked hopeless.

"We'll get it," said Dominic. "How about Noodles? How about Nose? Nostrum. Nobody. Nick. Nix. Nip. Not. Nut. Nit. Net. Nagasaki."

"No," said the elephant.

By the time they had gone through the letter A,

mentioning every word they could think of, they had reached the outskirts of Grandville and it was morning. They lay down in a field of newly cut hay and slept a long, refreshing sleep, from 5 a.m. till noon.

Now a big ripe sun floated in a wide, open sky, a beautiful day for a wedding. Dominic, Mwana, and Phineas bathed in a nearby brook. Mwana, using his trunk as a hose, sprayed the others and himself, and they all felt freshened. They had nothing to eat but grass. It was just as well, as they knew they would soon dine regally.

XV. The wedding was to take place right after sundown in the Crystal Ballroom. When the three new friends arrived in town, they learned where the ballroom was and parted company until wedding time, each of them needing to be alone for a while with his private thoughts and feelings before plunging into the big celebration.

Since Mwana couldn't wish himself into any money, Dominic gave him a gold piece to buy clothing suitable for a party. Phineas, fortunately, when he started his sleepwalk, had had the unconscious good sense to stuff some bills in the pocket of his nightshirt.

"See you at eight," said Dominic.

"Ta-ta," said Phineas.

"Don't forget to be there," said Mwana. "You're my only friends in this country." And each went off in a different direction.

After a little time walking and thinking, Dominic decided to smell out Grandville, his usual practice in towns he was visiting for the first time. He raced up and down avenues and alleys, rubbed himself against various poles, lamp-posts, cornerstones, and trees, inquired about the population and the town's history—how many members of each species it contained, the birth rate, when the town was founded and by whom, and why—looked up the oldest landmarks, smelled them carefully, asked about the climate at different times of the year, learned what the salary of schoolteachers was, and the price of tangerines, and soon knew more about the town than many who had spent a lifetime there. He saw banners announcing the wedding and overheard on a street corner some details of the lavish preparations. Barney certainly wasn't being stingy with the wealth he had come by so easily.

Dominic dropped into a barbershop run by a talkative pig named Angel Hoag, introduced himself, and sat in the chair.

"Not *the* Dominic!" said Mr. Hoag. Since Dominic was convinced he was the only Dominic around, and felt rather special even in his modest moments, he had to acknowledge that he was *the* Dominic, which of course he was.

"Happy to make your acquaintance. What can I do for you?" beamed Mr. Hoag. Dominic got a body shampoo, a hot towel on the ears and snout, and a very pleasant sprinkle of fur tonic. He gave Mr. Hoag

a gold piece for his troubles, and saying, "Keep the change. I hope I'll see you at the wedding," he left. After that, he bought a beautiful green velvet outfit in which he was sure of not being inconspicuous.

When Dominic, in the tailor's dressing room, was transferring his old clothes to the bandanna, he took out the doll he had recently found and sniffed it with intense pleasure. Again his heart was pierced with a yearning he didn't understand. He replaced the doll in the bandanna, and left, bidding good day to the tailor, a ram named Beerbohm Hemlock, who was also going to the wedding, Dominic being his last customer of the day.

There were still two hours to go. Dominic was now so impatient for the forthcoming event that he just had to keep moving. He hastened about the town once more, sniffing here and there, increasing his store of olfactory information, searching out whatever details of Grandville he had previously missed. Then he went to study the outskirts, circled the town a few times, this way and that, and finally sat down under a tree to rest briefly.

He remembered the doll again and his restlessness vanished. He unwrapped it and held it tenderly in his arms. The little puppy with the shoe-button eyes was quite soiled and damaged from years of handling. It was a run-of-the-mill, worn-with-use doll, and yet it held such magic for him. What was there about this lost plaything that he cared for so intensely? Why did it make him dream of things to come? Sitting with the doll in the rosy light of the setting sun, he knew he would be pleased with his future. He fell into a reverie and was no longer conscious of his surroundings or of passing time. Images of tender April flowers on soft hillsides, of limpid minty pools in sweet, purling brooks, of hushed, fern-filled, aromatic forests, of benign, embracing breezes and affectionate skies, of a peaceable world of happy creatures passed before his mind's eye.

Suddenly he realized he was late for the wedding. It was already night, with another unusual moon. He heard the town bells ring out nine o'clock—he hadn't noticed when they rang eight—and hastened into town.

XVI.

Dominic already knew Grandville very well. He went straight to the Crystal Ballroom, which was aglitter with lights, outside and in.

Without hesitation, he strode into the hall. His ears perked up at the din of revelry—the rollicking music, the rippling laughter, the hubbub of chattering voices. His eyes were delighted by the colourful clothes, the happy faces. His nose took note of various engaging smells—the smells of the many celebrators, the smell of the roses festooning the walls, the odours of eau de cologne, of tonics, lotions, perfumes and powders of all sorts that the guests had used lavishly, and the smells of delicious edibles prepared by the most skilful chefs of that region.

Dominic had not missed much, only the first hour—a time in which guests straggle in alone or in groups, are greeted, hang up their capes and other outer garments, powder their snouts in the powder room, are introduced to one another if they are not already acquainted, look each other over critically or admiringly, steal glances at themselves in any available mirror, and stand around shyly, making self-conscious remarks and wondering if the fun they anticipated will ever really begin.

All this preliminary discomfort and clumsiness was over when Dominic arrived. A lively gavotte was in progress and feet pounded to the accents of the music as partners swung about in hushed and heated happiness. Barney Swain, standing near the door like a good host, rushed to Dominic and embraced him warmly. He quickly produced his bride and presented her, saying, "*Here* is the dear dog we owe our great happiness to! Without him, all this would not be."

Pearl Sweeney, soon to be Swain, also embraced Dominic warmly. Looking at her, he understood Barney's adoration. She was as lovely as a wild boar can be, and glowed with health and happiness. Her beauty was set off by a gown of pink flowered silk damask.

Pearl looked into Dominic's eyes and said, "You are an angel. We will never forget you. My first child will be named Dominic, Dominica if a girl."

"I'll feel honoured," said Dominic, as always courtly with ladies. He was interrupted by a roll of drums announcing that the marriage ceremony was about to begin. Barney and Pearl excused themselves and went to the back of the hall.

Mwana, dressed in the robes of an African gentleman, came hurrying over to Dominic. "Thank goodness you're here," he said. "I felt so alone, not knowing anyone or how to behave in this society."

"Did you remember the magic word?"

"No," said Mwana sadly. "I'm giving my mind a rest. Maybe it will come to me of its own accord."

"Is it Asparagus?" asked Dominic.

"Nope," said Mwana.

The guests were grouping themselves on opposite

sides of the hall, with an aisle between them. The band struck up a dignified wedding march, both solemn and cheerful. Barney and Pearl moved with measured steps toward the altar. His eyes glowed with dedication. She looked lost in reveries of love.

The ceremony was performed by the Reverend Swoon, also a boar. When Barney spoke the words, "With this ring I thee wed," a fervent hoarseness in his voice, he placed the wedding ring in Pearl's nose.

They were pronounced husband and wife, and there were cheers and other sounds of exultation from the spectators. Everyone came forward with congratulations and then took to kissing the bride, while Barney stood by proudly, happy for those who had the privilege, this once, of embracing his lovely Pearl.

The kissing and congratulating finally over, the crowd yielded to hunger, encouraged by the heavenly aromas that drifted from the kitchen. The food was

carried in on silver trays and arrayed on long buffet tables while the band played food music. Among the artfully prepared dishes were cranberries with walnut sauce, grass à la française, cheese soufflé with acorns, new potatoes with garlic sauce, bones marinated in Burgundy, oat fritters, pâté of sunflower seeds, stuffed watermelon, daisy salad, clover jelly, and orange doodle. There was also plenty to drink—dandelion wine, mushroom beer, ale made from nuts and alfalfa, honeysuckle juice, sweet and sour water, bark brandy. The gaily dressed guests ate standing, moving among the tables, bowing, joking, congratulating, exchanging pleasantries.

Mrs. Matilda Fox, spearing a nut cutlet, spotted Dominic in the crowd and waddled swiftly to him with her five goslings. The grateful, fond goose hugged and kissed him. He hugged and kissed her and then kissed the five children, in alphabetical order so as not to offend any of them. They gabbled with joy and all tried to get his attention at once. Mwana came over with a plate of bananas and devilled asparagus and was introduced to the Foxes. The goslings stared because they had never seen a live elephant before. They had only seen pictures and were puzzled because they had been told that elephants are enormous.

"Is Banana the word?" Dominic whispered to Mwana, looking at his plate.

"I've tried all the fruits and vegetables," he answered. "It's none of those."

Dominic noticed that Elijah Hogg, the jackass, had turned up and was being introduced all around.

Mrs. Fox began telling Dominic about some of the things she had bought with the treasure he'd given her—things for herself and for the children—a boat for their pond, a diving board, a large sun umbrella, croquet mallets, etc. Dominic listened attentively, but he was also listening attentively to everything else that went on, all eyes, all ears, all nose, alert to the whole hustle and bustle, the stir and movement of the crowd.

Suddenly the lights were dimmed and flaming desserts, pumpkin jubilee, were brought in by a procession of waiters. A cheer burst from the crowd as fireworks shot from all the plates simultaneously. Then the lights were turned up again. The children began chasing one another under and around the tables. The band played a tarantella. Many danced, wheeling with happy abandon. Skirts swirled, feet tapped and skittered on the polished floor.

Dominic glowed with pleasure. He was brought over to meet relatives of the bride and groom—Herman Swann, Maribelle Swen, Mervyn Swyn, Caroline Swahan and her children. Dominic danced the remainder of the tarantella with Matilda Fox. He danced so well she applauded him with enthusiastic wings. He circled and bowed, inspired by her feminine compliments.

Elijah Hogg danced with the bride's cousin, Maribelle. His hoofs clattered on the glistening boards. A toast to Mr. and Mrs. Swain was proposed. There was another roll of drums, a chattering of tambourines, a clash of cymbals. Drinks were passed around. "To the eternal happiness of the Swains!" someone shouted, raising a glass of mango brandy. There were many quick cries of "Ditto!", the clinking of many glasses, the downing of many drinks

"Is the word Loganberry?" Dominic asked Mwana.

"I tried *all* the fruits and vegetables," he answered.

Then a group of madcap acrobats came tumbling and somersaulting in, and room was made for them in the centre of the floor. Two powerful pigs stood shoulder to shoulder. Two strong dogs raced up the backs of the powerful pigs and stood ready on their heads. A monkey climbed to the top of this living structure while balancing a spinning plate on the tip of a staff.

Dominic, who was getting more and more excited by this feat, grabbed a handy window pole and vaulted himself onto the monkey's back. From there he shinnied up the staff, tossed the plate aside, and stood balanced on one foot on the tip. There was great applause, an ovation; the acrobats leaped to the ground, and Dominic raced around the room with them, doing cartwheels and flips.

At this point Lemuel Wallaby, the turtle, tottered in, asking if the marriage ceremony had yet taken place. He was disappointed to learn that that event was long over, and started toward the bride and groom, who were now receiving guests bearing presents. Dominic apologized for forgetting to bring anything, but Barney and Pearl reminded him that he had already given them more than enough.

The band struck up a dance again, this time a waltz. Dominic was moved to play and sat in with his piccolo. He played so dazzlingly that the other musicians muted their instruments to let his enchanting sounds prevail.

At this point three members of the Doomsday Gang—two wildcats and a ferret—came into the ballroom wearing fancy clothes and acting as though they had been invited. They were heading toward the heap of gifts when they were discovered by Matilda Fox, who cried out in indignation. The music stopped, and so did the dancing. Dominic leaped from the bandstand, ran for the cloakroom, and reappeared with his spear, whereupon the impostors ambled rather quickly to the door and made a sudden exit. Dominic gave short chase.

He was roundly cheered on his return. He then played a piccolo solo with brilliant embellishments. By now Lemuel Wallaby had reached the newlyweds to offer them his congratulations and his regrets at being late. Champagne was served. A skunk raised his glass and shouted, "To the Swains and their progeny. Long may they prosper!" Everyone drank.

More champagne was served. A rabbit shouted, "I now proclaim the eternal brotherhood of the entire animal kingdom!" Everyone drank again.

Dominic was feeling an immense well-being and overwhelming goodwill toward everything that lived. "Here's to unending love!" he shouted. Everyone drank once more.

Mwana turned up at his side and Dominic asked: "Is the word Whisky?"

"It's not an alcoholic beverage," said Mwana. "I've tried them all. I've tried fruits, vegetables, beverages, flowers, articles of furniture, names of minerals, and I don't have it."

Barney Swain was now up on the bandstand, which had been furnished with a red velvet curtain so it could serve as a stage. "I have the great pleasure to announce," he said in a loud voice, "that the Pumpkin Hollow Players, as fine a company of actors as ever there was, are putting on for our entertainment a play which has been especially prepared for this occasion. The name of the play is *The Exploits of Dominic*. If you'll arrange yourselves so you all have a clear view of the stage, the curtain will go up and the play will begin."

Everyone craned to look at Dominic. He was embarrassed, an unusual condition for him. "Exploits?" he thought. "I haven't had any exploits. Nothing worth making a play about."

The curtain went up and revealed "Dominic" walking along a road with his spear over his shoulder. There was no dog among the Pumpkin Hollow Players, so the part of Dominic was being played by a cat, who gave a poor imitation of his movements, slinking where Dominic strode. This annoyed Dominic. The cat wore a mask with a large black snout and pendant ears.

A hole had been prepared in the stage, into which the cat—that is, "Dominic"—fell, and a scene followed in which he was mocked and tormented by the Doomsday Gang. But instead of escaping the way Dominic actually had, the play-Dominic fought his way out of the hole, killed two of the villains with his spear, spared the life of another, who promised to reform, and routed the rest. When he was attacked after digging up Bartholomew Badger's treasure, the play showed him defeating the entire gang single-handed.

"That isn't the way it was at all," said Dominic to Mwana, who was standing at his side. "By the way, the word isn't Cutlets, is it?"

"No. Sorry," Mwana said. "Thank you for trying."

Another "exploit" of Dominic's was being shown on the stage. The villains were hanging up Matilda Fox, played by a rabbit, and Dominic charged in, mounted on Elijah Hogg, played by a pig, dispersing the villains and killing three of them.

"That's not the way it was at all," murmured

Dominic as the curtain went down and the guests turned and applauded him rather than the play.

Then suddenly, shockingly, flames were swarming up the curtain. The actors came rushing off the open sides of the stage squawking and howling, and guests were grabbing up their children and making for the exits.

"Water!" someone shouted. "Get water!" Fires were starting up all over the hall. Flame tore through some of the windows, some of the doors. The room echoed with panic-stricken screams. The exits were all aflame now, and black smoke was rolling through the room, engulfing everything. There were cries for "Air!", hysterical shoving and pushing.

Dominic raced around sizing up the situation, trying excitedly to calm the others. Some of the animals beat at the flames with their coats. There were more cries of "Water!", more cries of "Air!"

The only available water was in the kitchen, but the kitchen was on fire too. Barney Swain tried to fight his way in there, but only got the bristles on his face badly singed. He hurried back to protect his bride. Someone tried spilling champagne on the flames, but it did no good. Brandy was worse—it made the fire burn more fiercely.

Mothers embraced their children. Some were crying. Matilda Fox's goslings huddled under her wings, pitifully honking. Lemuel Wallaby, moving faster than usual, began working his way toward the nearest door, undeterred by animals stepping on his shell.

Dominic grabbed Mwana and held him tight. "You *must* remember the magic word!"

"I can't!" said Mwana.

"You *can!*" said Dominic. "Try. Don't get excited. Relax and, presto, you'll have it."

"P R E S T O!" screamed Mwana. "That's it! That's the word! *Presto,*" he said. "Presto, let the fire cease! Presto!"

All at once there was **no fire**. There were no flames, no smoke, no sputtering sparks, no hissing wood. Everyone stood transfixed, dumbfounded. Had this really happened? Had they really witnessed such a

marvel? Yes, indeed. They had. A chorus of sighs filled the hall.

"Put things back as they were," said Dominic to Mwana.

"Presto," said Mwana. "Let it be as it was before the fire. Presto." And everything was exactly as it had been before the fire. Not exactly, because the crowd was no longer thinking about the play and applauding Dominic.

Mwana, by now having had enough of the pleasures and the pains of this new country, said goodbye to Dominic, left regards for the others, wished himself back home in Africa, and vanished.

Dominic mounted the stage and rapped the haft of his spear on the boards for attention. "Our good friend Mwana Bhomba remembered a magic word in the nick of time," he said, "and that's how our lives have been saved."

Everyone began bubbling with conversation.

Dominic rapped for attention again. "Now is the time to deal properly with the Doomsday Gang, who, as we all well know, set that terrible fire. We surely equal them in number. Let's go after them and teach them a lesson! To arms! Follow me, my nose will lead the way!"

XVII. All the males at the wedding, including the bridegroom, took up whatever weapons they could find in the Crystal Ballroom: window poles, chair legs, table legs, canes, skewers from the kitchen, long ladles, rolling pins, brooms, mops, and even fruits and vegetables that could be used as missiles—prickly pineapples, heavy melons, coconuts. Dominic preceded them through the main portal, holding aloft his trusty spear.

It was a motley army, dressed as the soldiers were in festive clothes and brandishing their makeshift weapons, that erupted from the brilliantly illuminated ballroom into another enchanted night. The peaceful moon shed its benign light on the horde of enraged animals going after their enemies. To Dominic the air reeked with the vile aroma of the villains.

Guided by this, he led the way out of town, over the fields, across a rocky stream, and into a forest where the moonlight filtered through a maze of leaves. Suddenly he held up his spear, and the army halted. The stench of the Doomsday Gang was becoming intolerable. "Proceed slowly," Dominic whispered, and he moved forward with caution, his army at his back.

Soon they saw campfires set in a clearing, and there, sitting around the fires, were the various villains, making ugly jokes and laughing raucously, their fangs lighted up by the flames. Some were rolling on the ground screeching guffaws, some were slapping their neighbours' backs in relish of their maliciousness. Their leader, the fox, was dancing about, reminding them loudly of incidents at the Crystal Ballroom fire and prancing up and down as if trying to stamp out his own seizures of laughter. They were all sure they had just achieved their most glorious moment of infamy. They thought the damage must be enormous; and imagining the pain and unhappiness of the victims made their cups of joy run over.

Dominic's army watched in horrified fascination. Could creatures really be that wicked? Apparently they could. "At them!" shouted Dominic. His army came tearing through the trees, swinging their assorted cudgels right and left, powerful with righteous rage. Dominic thrust and slashed with his spear.

The hilarious mood of the villains vanished. Taken

by surprise and unarmed, some fled, even through the campfires, kicking sparks and embers in all directions and singeing their fur. Some fell to their knees begging for mercy, which was not forthcoming. Others managed to grab their weapons and fight back. Those who ran were chased and soundly cudgelled, and pelted with fruits and rocks and clods of earth as they disappeared. Those who fought back were finally routed, with Dominic's army after them, dispensing farewell thumps and thwacks.

But Dominic had been injured. The avenging army, returning to the clearing, found him on the ground, unconscious, his spear at his side. The villains had concentrated their fury on Dominic, since they hated him the most. He had been dealt some damaging blows, a few of which came from his own cohorts trying to help him.

Seeing their leader so still, they feared he might be dead, and as they moved toward him, some began to weep. Barney Swain listened to Dominic's heart. It was beating strongly and steadily. He assured the others that Dominic was very much alive, though apparently injured.

They made a stretcher out of some sticks laced together with belts, covered it with grass and leaves, and carefully laid Dominic on this bed of greenery. They carried him back into Grandville, careful not to jolt or disturb him in any way.

Lying unconscious, Dominic imagined he was still

fighting the enemy, and muttered, "There!" or "Take that, you fiend!" as he thrust an imaginary spear at one scoundrel or another.

He regained consciousness early in the morning and found himself lying on a silken bed in a room fragrant with flowers, in the plush new home of Mr. and Mrs. Barney Swain. Seated at his side was Dr. Fetlock, a horse. Barney and Pearl were there in the room, Matilda Fox and her children were there, and others as well. They were all gazing at Dominic with concern.

"Where am I?" were his first words. He was told where he was. "What happened?" he then asked. He was told what had happened. "Oh," he said, "I seem to remember." The physician then introduced himself and told Dominic he had been badly bruised but no bones were broken.

"I hurt all over," said Dominic. Dr. Fetlock took Dominic's pulse, thoughtfully listened to his heart, looked into his ears and throat, verified that his nose was cool, as it should be, and recommended a few days of bed rest and something to eat immediately.

Barney Swain went out on the balcony to announce to the crowd gathered outside that their hero would be all right; and they, after waiting up anxiously all through the night, cheered and went home at last to sleep. Dominic had a meal of some of the good food remaining from the wedding.

"How happy we are that you're well!" Matilda Fox.

"We were so worried," said Pearl Swain, a a day ago and now a married woman.

Barney Swain touched Dominic's arm and gave h a look that said much. The five goslings swarme around the bed and gabbled gaily. Dominic, feeling very much loved, soon fell asleep again. The others tiptoed out.

Long hours later Dominic woke up. He was feeling fine, fit and eager to be out in the world where everything was waiting to happen. He also thought the Swains should be left to themselves so they could begin enjoying their married life. Careful to make no noise, he got out of bed. He packed his bandanna, put on his beret, and wrote a note thanking everyone for their care and concern, adding that he hoped to see them all in the future. He left the house unseen by anyone. It was twilight.

XVIII.

Dominic felt glad to be on the road again. He strolled along, watching the day convert to darkness and reviewing the events of the previous night and all that had happened since he'd left home to seek his fortune. The alligator-witch had certainly been right. Life wasn't dull along this road. Fighting the bad ones in the world was a necessary and gratifying experience. Being happy among the good ones was, of course, even more gratifying. But one could not be happy among the good ones unless one fought the bad ones. He felt he was serving some important and useful purpose.

Then he began wondering what was still in store for him, and without thinking he hastened his steps as if to find out faster. Soon he realized he was not as fit as he thought. He began to feel his injuries and he was exhausted.

It was yet another night of magical moonlight, as mysterious and beautiful as the nights preceding it. Dominic was now in some woods rich with summer fragrance: the delicious, soul-soothing smells of growing things, the smell of warm earth, the smells the air had brought from other places—the sea, meadows, gardens. He made himself a bed in some woodland grass, the kind that grows soft as down under trees, where he was neighboured by clusters of wild forest flowers. No sooner did this tired dog lay down his head and heave a thorough sigh than he was dreaming. Moonshine bathed the sleeping Dominic, and there was moonshine in his dream.

He wasn't experiencing this dream in the usual way. It was as if he were sitting alone in a theatre watching a play whose hero was himself. The Dominic on the stage was running away from an alligator-witch because he didn't want to hear the rest of his life story, not even the next episode. The Dominic sitting in the theatre was afraid the witch might catch the Dominic on the stage. But that Dominic wearied of running away and turned to wait for the witch and let her talk, but she wasn't there any more. Then he realized he was badly hurt. He was aware of pains all over his body. Now he was lying down and someone was making him feel better, soothing his hurts, causing them to dissolve and disappear. He couldn't see this someone and yet he somehow knew that she was dearly beautiful. Who was she? He didn't know

her, yet he knew her well. And then they were walking close together, and the Dominic sitting in the dream theatre was wishing he were the Dominic on the stage . . .

While Dominic was absorbed in this dream, all was not peaceful around him. The remnants of the Doomsday Gang had regrouped since the previous night and had discovered his whereabouts in the woods, one of the ferrets having ferreted him out. They were silently closing in on this spear-carrying dog who persistently spoiled their evil designs. Before he turned up, they had been the undisputed terrors of the territory, most of their mischief meeting with success. They hated Dominic with all their hearts,

and their hearts were capable of drastic hatred. Now they intended to subtract him from the sum of existing things.

There he lay, innocently dreaming and so exhausted that his ears and nose, usually keen even when he was asleep, failed to alert him. The villains were creeping closer on all sides, eyes gleaming with malice, variously armed, even their sharp claws unsheathed.

Dominic dreamed on. Now they were flagrantly close, the would-be killers. A few had raised their deadly knives and clubs. But suddenly they stood like bewildered statues, listening. From all around them, from the whole woods, they heard voices—calling, echoing, re-echoing, repeating Dominic's name. "Domi-nic! *Dominic!* D O M I N I C ! Dominic! Wake up. *Wake up, Dominic!"*

It was the trees. The trees were calling him. They began to writhe and bend and wave their limbs as if they were yielding under a heavy storm, and made terrible, creaking, cracking sounds.

News of the bright, brave, generous dog named Dominic had been spreading through the forest for some time, and the trees had come to love him. More than that, they had become impatient with standing around in silent tableau, doing nothing but looking grand and storing up resentment, indignation, and grief while all the evil-doing, the doom-delivering, of the Doomsday Gang went on.

Now that Dominic, dear dog, was about to be killed in their midst, in the very heart of the woods, the trees were moved to speak out, to break their lifelong silence. Dominic heard and woke and saw it all, the gang posed about him, weapons upraised, but petri-fied with terror. And at that moment the surrounding trees bent toward the villains, saying, "For shame! F I E !"

Scared out of their wits entirely, the gang bolted in every possible direction, seeking the quickest way out of the woods. They were never heard from again, not as a gang, or as individual malefactors. The terror of this experience, the condemnation from the lords of the hitherto silent vegetable kingdom, had penetrated

to their souls. Convinced that Nature itself could no longer abide their destructive, criminal ways, they each slunk about separately, making efforts to reform and get into Nature's good graces again, as every wanton one of them had been in his original childhood.

Dominic, in awe and gratitude, knelt and made obeisance to the trees. A responsive breeze rustled in their branches, a light sighing. For a while he wandered through the woods, lovingly touching many a tree. Small birds that should have been asleep were singing. He was happy.

XIX. Later that night he came out of the woods and found himself in a garden. At the edge of the garden was a marble fountain whose jets rose gently, curved gracefully outward, and fell like soft rain into a pool, crimson-lined and full of goldfish. In the magic moonlight, every droplet of spray glistened like a pearl.

Dominic gazed at the fountain, feeling his soul washed by the sight of it, enjoying the coolness that caressed him. Suddenly he smelled that smell again, the scent that so intrigued him, that brought him premonitions of unknown joy. The smell of the doll was in the air of the garden.

A resplendent peacock appeared from the other side of the fountain, and bowed before Dominic. The iridescent hues of his spreading tail, the lustrous ovals, were quite clear in the light of the moon. Even the feathers' delicate fringing was plainly visible. The spray from the fountain reflected the peacock's colours in dim rainbows. Behind the peacock, behind the fountain, were tiers of multicoloured flowers, Dominic suddenly noticed.

"Welcome to the garden, Dominic," said the peacock graciously.

"Thank you," said Dominic. "You have such a beautiful tail. It makes the fountain more beautiful, and the flowers, and they do the same for your tail."

The peacock bowed again and rustled his feathers proudly, as if he were fluttering a fan.

"Whose garden is this?" Dominic asked.

"This is an enchanted garden," said the peacock, "and I am its seneschal. No one but you has ever found his way here. You are the first visitor."

"I feel honoured," said Dominic quietly.

"You are extremely special," said the peacock.

Dominic didn't know what to say next. He looked around. "I've never seen such beautiful flowers!" he exclaimed.

"Yes," said the peacock. "They never grow old, they never die."

"Not even in winter?" Dominic asked.

"It is never winter here," said the peacock. "It may be winter all around, blizzards may rage, but it is never ever winter in this spot. I can reach out and touch the snow, feel its freezing coldness, and still be standing where it's always summer."

"Amazing!" said Dominic. Though he had seen so many marvels, his sense of wonder never waned.

"Let me show you around," said the peacock, "as long as you're here. I've had no one to talk to for many a year, though, oddly, I haven't been lonesome. I've spent a good deal of time admiring my tail. It's nice to have someone else admire it for a change, to hear it praised."

"What are those flowers?" asked Dominic, pointing at a row of very large blossoms of deep crimson and royal violet speckled with white.

"Touch one," said the peacock. Dominic did and there was a delicate ringing of bells.

"Touch another." He did. And now there was music, a lovely, light melody as if breezes were playing on a wind instrument. He touched other flowers and there was orchestration—strings, soft brasses, reeds, light percussion. Dominic felt called upon to join in. Under the golden moon he played his golden piccolo, and he and the flowers understood one another and rose to greater and greater heights of loveliness.

The peacock spread his gorgeous tail about him and listened. Dominic did not know how long he played. And when the music was over, there was no stopping him; he had to sit down on his haunches and yield to some deeply felt howling, not harsh, pent-up howls this time, but soft, yodelling ululations, expressive of feelings that affirmed his presence in an

ancient yet young universe. The peacock attended respectfully till Dominic was done.

Having expressed his feelings, Dominic looked around once more. He noticed a building towards the back of the garden. It looked like a miniature palace. It had a tiny dome surrounded by tiny turrets, and arched windows and an arched doorway, all profusely encrusted with coloured gems. "What is that?" he asked. It was as if he were being introduced to these marvels one at a time, in some predetermined order.

"That?" said the peacock. "That is what this garden is the setting for, that is why this fountain is here and why I am here. And that is really why you are here, if I'm not mistaken."

"May I go in?" asked Dominic.

"Indeed you may. But tiptoe, for someone is asleep in there who has been asleep for many years."

Dominic approached the entrance, shivering with anticipation. Among the aromas of the garden flowers, there stood out clearly the scent he had first encountered on the doll he carried in his bandanna. The door gave way easily and Dominic found himself in a room where candles flickered and moonlight streamed through stained-glass windows, illuminating a canopied bed where the most beautiful dog he had ever seen lay sleeping. She was black and shimmered in patterns of luminous purple, yellow, green, blue, and carmine from the windows. She looked unreal.

Shyly—how odd for Dominic to be so shy—he touched her. Instantly she was awake, gazing at him with large black eyes. "Are you the one?" she asked.

"I think I am," said Dominic.

"Do you have the doll?"

"Yes, I do," said Dominic.

"You're the one," she said.

They looked a long time at each other; and both were happy with what they saw. It was preordained. No doubt the witch-alligator would have predicted it if Dominic had allowed her to.

"How long have I been here?" asked the beauty.

"I don't know," said Dominic. "But the peacock in the garden says many years."

"Peacock? I didn't know there was a peacock. Yes, I guess I have been here many years. Do I still look young?"

"Yes," said Dominic. "Yes, you do. You're beautiful."

"I was told I wouldn't grow older while I was asleep, that I'd remain unchanged until the right one came along to break the spell. Just like Sleeping Beauty."

"What is your name?" Dominic asked.

"Evelyn," she said. "That doll you have was mine when I was a child. I loved that doll and always had it with me. One day, when I'd grown up and decided I was no longer a child, I threw it away. I remember I was standing in a field thinking about life and about myself and about growing up. I became eager for the future and I felt the doll chained me to the past. So I got rid of it. But even while I was walking away from that field, I began to have doubts. I had been happy in my puppy days. Would I be a happy grown-up? I wandered about in a sort of trance, until I found myself standing in front of an alligator-witch."

"I should have known!" Dominic exclaimed. "The alligator-witch."

Evelyn nodded and continued. " 'What's wrong?' she asked me, and I told her.

" 'Come with me,' the witch said, and she took me by the paw. I followed her without questioning, without having an impulse to question. She brought me here. 'You are going to sleep,' she said, 'maybe for a long time. Someone will find your doll, and whoever finds it will also find you, you can be sure of that. Now you must sleep,' she said, and I obediently went to sleep. I was under her spell. I had no thought of doing anything but what she suggested. Anyway, here you are, the one who found my doll. The witch was right."

"The witch was right," Dominic agreed.

"May I have my doll?" said Evelyn. Dominic gave her the doll, and she hugged it like a long-lost child. "Let's leave right away," she said. "I've been here so long, I want to be out in the world again."

Dominic realized he was at the beginning of a great new adventure.

"Let's go," he said.

Together they left the little palace.

Alan Garner

THE WEIRDSTONE OF BRISINGAMEN
THE MOON OF GOMRATH
ELIDOR
THE OWL SERVICE

When Alan Garner's first book, *The Weirdstone of Brisingamen*, was published he was hailed by reviewers as a great new writer. *The Weirdstone* and its sequel *The Moon of Gomrath* are fantasies of striking imagination and power set around Alderley Edge in Cheshire where Alan Garner lives.

With the publication of *The Owl Service* Alan Garner received both the Guardian Award and the Carnegie Medal. Set in Wales, the story describes the reawakening of an ancient legend of jealousy and destruction which threatens to live again in Alison, Roger and Gwyn.

Alan Garner has been described in the *Times Educational Supplement* as 'one of the most exciting writers for young people today. He is producing work with strong plot structure, perceptive characterisation and vivid language. Furthermore, there is in his writing a basic integrity within which the poetic imagination may have free rein. It is a combination of qualities that creates literature that will be read and read again.'

Charley

JOAN G. ROBINSON

'I don't want Charley. You know that . . .'

So Auntie Louie didn't want her, nor did Aunt Emm. Well, she could do without them, too.

So Charley runs away to live in a field. Her bed is a bit hard and there are earwigs in her supper, but the henhouse is familiar and comforting. She decides she is going to be all right until the sun goes down . . . Perhaps she *should* move closer to Aunt Louie's house just in case of an earthquake or a deluge . . .

Charley's week in the woods is a mixture of joy and terror, magic and misery, and from it all she gains a new understanding of herself and those she thought didn't love her.

When Marnie Was There by Joan G. Robinson is also in Lions.

The Phantom Tollbooth

NORTON JUSTER

'It seems to me that almost everything is a waste of time,' Milo remarks as he walks dejectedly home from school. But his glumness soon turns to surprise when he unwraps a mysterious package marked ONE GENUINE PHANTOM TOLLBOOTH. Once through the Phantom Tollboth Milo has no more time to be bored for before him lies the strange land of the Kingdom of Wisdom and a series of even stranger adventures when he meets the watchdog Tock who ticks, King Azaz the unabridged the unhappy ruler of Dictionopolis, Faintly Macabre the not so wicked Which, the Whether Man and the threadbare Excuse, among a collection of the most logically illogical characters ever met on this side or that side of reality.

For readers of ten upwards.

Little Lord Fauntleroy

FRANCES HODGSON BURNETT

'I should rather not be an earl. None of the other boys are earls. Can't I *not* be one?' said Cedric on learning of his sudden inheritance of wealth and a title. Undaunted by the prospect of becoming a lord, he bravely leaves his poor but happy life with his mother and friends in New York, and sails for England to face life with his lonely and gouty old grandfather, the Earl of Dorincourt, in his stately turreted castle.

Little Lord Fauntleroy was first published in 1885 and since then has become one of the best loved rags to riches stories of all time.

For nine-year-olds and up.

The Haunted Mountain

MOLLIE HUNTER

Long ago in the wild Highlands of Scotland lived McAllister, a big handsome man as strong as a pine tree. But so stubborn was he to run his own life that he defied the sidhe, the evil fairy folk. Now this was a reckless thing to do, for the sidhe seeking revenge, imprisoned him inside the massive mountain of Ben MacDui. The sidhe, however, had not reckoned on the determination of Fergus his son, who gradually grew to realise that unless he rescued his father, the Great Grey Man of the haunted mountain would keep him forever.

Mollie Hunter won a Scottish Arts Council Award in 1973 for this powerful fantasy for nine-year-olds and upwards.

The Little Captain

PAUL BIEGEL

The little captain set sail in his brave ship, the *Neversink*, with Podgy, Marinka, and timid Thomas in search of the island of Evertaller. There they would grow into giants overnight and *never* have to go to school again.

The *Neversink* sailed over the wide, wild sea towards the Stone Dragon gates. Suddenly the dragons sprang into life to seize the little boat in their claws! And Evertaller wasn't *quite* what they'd expected either . . . So on they ventured, this time to the mysterious island. Timid Thomas disappeared – carried off by something which left only handprints in the sand! And everywhere wild animals lurked. But the little captain and his crew met the scariest weirdest adventure of all in the Misty City . . .

The King of the Copper Mountains is also a Lion.

For eight-year-olds and upwards.